Potholes and Paris

Potholes and Paris

Also by Maureen Mendelowitz and published by Ginninderra Press

The Rock
Alone Not Lonely
What Have You Done?

Maureen Mendelowitz

Potholes and Paris

Potholes and Paris
ISBN 978 1 76109 014 1
Copyright © Maureen Mendelowitz 2020
Cover image: *Art in Glass* by Taryn Tollman
Design: Robyn Zeller

First published 2020 by
GINNINDERRA PRESS
PO Box 3461 Port Adelaide 5015
www.ginninderrapress.com.au

From Julian –
As we lie beneath a clear Cape sky
Or tread a path beneath a copper sun…

For Julian
Always

It wasn't much more than a railway siding. An office, a wooden bench, a faded name on a board between poles. A large storage shed with a corrugated-iron roof.

On the opposite side of the line a ramshackle house. A few patched cottages.

A bony child kicking a ball. A skulking dog. A woman with a *doekie* on her head, hanging washing.

A stony road.

Suspended dust.

*

She came on the goods train with a strapped suitcase and a bag, a woman in a brown coat, her hair tied back, her face devoid of colour. She walked along the broken paving, past the shed and onto the uneven road, leaning sideways because of her suitcase.

This must be the Main Road, she thought, remembering the instructions. Down this road and third to the left into Bluegum Street. 'Go past the *algemene handelaar*, the post office/barber/hairdresser, and the house with a white picket fence and tables and chairs on the stoep – Marie's place – where they serve tea and scones. Says on the gate – Refreshments served.'

The sun was warm through her coat, the air dry, the day windless. She stopped to change the suitcase from one hand to the other and hitched the bag onto her shoulder. Turned into Bluegum Street, passing houses slumped behind wire fences, lawns with dry brown patches, a crowded bush of yellow daisies and an old fig tree, its trunk painted white.

The pavement was rough with rocks and stones. Her bag weighed down on her thin frame. Again she changed hands. The house she'd rented was the last in the road, a white house with a red tin roof. There was no number. The last house in the road opposite the veld. It would be un-locked. The key to the front door was on the mantelpiece, under a vase.

Polished surfaces from the steps and stoep reflected sunlight. Through the door, solid and plain with a brass knocker shaped like a anchor, was the lounge, a square room with white walls, its wide windows covered by thick maroon curtains. A maroon couch in leatherette against one wall faced two matching chairs with wooden arms and legs. In front of the couch was a coffee table, behind one of the chairs a standing lamp. A fireplace. A set of fire irons. A vase on the mantelpiece.

Marina shrugged out of her coat, pulled the curtains and opened the windows. Light and air flooded the room. It's a nice room, she thought.

She dragged her bags over the wooden strip floor to the bedroom. A bed was made with crisp white sheets and puffed pillows. A yellowwood cupboard took up most of one wall.

I should unpack, she thought, glancing at her bags.

Instead, she ran a bath, left her clothes in a heap on the floor, stepped into the steaming water and lay back, her eyes closed, the ends of her tied hair floating. She told herself not to fall asleep.

A shaft of sunlight streamed through the window. Except for the occasional drip of the tap, there was silence.

*

The sun was sinking behind the mountain and a cold wind blew. Reflected crimson from the sky flushed the walls into hues of blushing rose. For a moment, she wondered where she was.

Shivering in the cool water, she pulled the plug, and, feeling unsteady, held onto the sides of the bath and waited for a few moments. Carefully she stepped out, rubbed herself vigorously with a large towel and padded to the bedroom. From her suitcase, she pulled out warm pyjamas, an old woollen gown and fleecy-lined slippers.

The house was cold. Bare floors reflected cold and cold air drafted in from under the doors. She would have liked to light a fire, to warm some soup, to make hot chocolate. But there was no food in the kitchen.

In the black sky, the moon was a hugely brilliant orb and the stars glittered. She climbed into the bed in her gown, ate the remaining biscuits she'd brought for the train, pulled the covers over her, and, shivering from a chill that came from within her, lay quite still listening to the silence, waiting for sleep to come.

She awoke to a knock on the door. There was a pause. It started again. Pushing her hair from her face, and her feet into her slippers, she opened the door to a tall and brawny man in a stained leather hat, with a smile that brought crows' lines to his candid blue gaze.

'Frederick van Rooyen.' He extended a large freckled hand, taking in her dishevelled appearance and confusion. 'Sorry. I think I woke you.'

'It's OK.' She pushed her hair back and tried to smile against the burning light at the outline of the man. 'I overslept…'

'*Nee, man.* Don't worry. It's *maar* early. I jus' came by to see if you're OK. If you have everything…'

'Thank you. Yes. Everything's OK. It's a nice house. Thank you.'

'*Nee, man. Dis goed.* Well, if you need anything, food or something, you can buy it all at the shop. My sister will help you. Annalise.'

'Thanks. I will go later.'

'Also, there's firewood in the shed at the back. You can make a fire. It can be very cold at night.' He watched her wan face, her tired dark eyes, the dark circles.

'Thank you. As you say, it was cold last night.' She shifted nervously and folded her arms around her thin form.

'OK. Well, I'll be off, then. Let me know if there's anything you need. You can always leave a message at the shop.' He noted her bony wrists, her large square hands.

'I will. And thank you for coming.'

He touched the brim of his hat. '*Totsiens, Mevrou.*'

'Marina. My name's Marina.'

'Marina. An' you can call me Fred.' He smiled, his eyes wrinkling, his teeth stained. There was bristle on his chin.

'OK, Fred. Thanks again…'

'OK, then. Bye.'

'Bye.'

For a moment she watched his large frame shamble down the path. Then quietly closed the door.

*

He told his sister, 'Very thin. She needs some meat on her.'

*

Through the window, the haze was ash blue. Shrubs, scrub and thorn trees blended into the winter light of the plateau, stretching to the mauve backdrop of the distant mountains.

A bird called – *whowho who whooo.*

She thought she saw a hare quiver and dart.

She opened the whitewashed rooms to the outside. Throughout the house, the desert air filtered. Light struck the floorboards and the yellow-wood wardrobe turned gold. It looked almost empty, her few clothes lost in its capacious space.

She showered quickly and dressed. She was hungry. She craved a cup of strong coffee. She needed to get to Annalise. She needed to shop.

The day felt lazy although it had hardly begun. The haze had lifted and the sky was now a sharp and seamless blue. She who walked fast, who was always in a hurry, found herself slowing down, her pace matching the sluggish day. Her gaze wandered from the sunburnt roof of a house to a swing hanging on ropes in a garden. There was a straggling rose bush. A rickety table. A truck in a driveway, its front wheels missing. She heard a baby cry. She thought she saw a curtain twitch.

The day was warm. A dog padded to a gate and barked half-heartedly, before lying down on heated stones.

She wondered who lived in the houses. What they did…

She walked past Marie's place and saw the sign 'Refresments served'. The 'h' was missing. A tantalising smell of baking came to her. Wonderful, she thought, savouring the thought of scones rising in an oven.

Annalise's shop was long and dim, the only light from the front door and an oblong of sunshine from a door at the rear of the building. Behind the wooden counter, behind an old-fashioned till, Annalise was filling glass jars with boiled sweets. She automatically fluffed her blonde hair and smiled her cherry-lipped, white-toothed, blue-eyed smile, her face glowing in the grey light.

'Morning.'

'Morning, *Mevrou.* I'm Marina. Marina Zetterling.'

'I know. I know.' Her voice had laughter and song. 'You're staying in Frederick's house, not so?'

'Yes.'

'I'm Annalise. His sister.' The hand she held out was white and plump, sparkling with jewels and red nail polish. 'I'm pleased to meet you.'

'Thank you.'

'What can I help you with?'

Marina tried to smile. 'Everything. My cupboard is bare.'

They walked down the length of the shop, along the crammed shelves. Tea, coffee, sugar, honey, berry jam, tinned beans. From the refrigerator, bottled milk, butter, cheese, bacon and sausages. From crates in the shadows, a bunch of carrots, a few onions, a couple of potatoes, some tomatoes and a cabbage, red and green apples, bright oranges, two bananas.

'Dora will help you,' smiled Annalise.

'Oh, and bread, I forgot the bread…and eggs.'

'Bread you get from Marie. She makes the bread. Fresh. Every day. Except Sunday. Also the eggs. She sells eggs. She's got chickens behind the house. Is there anything else?'

'I've just remembered… Do you sell blankets? It's so cold at night.'

'Blankets? Yes. I've got just the thing for you. A blanket made from

Merino wool. Very warm. It's big. You can fold it double. It'll keep you warm. I use one. It's wonderful. Really lovely on the bed. How's this?' She shook out a large blanket in a shade of blue.

'That's perfect. Thank you.'

'That's OK. Now. Let's get Dora. Dora…' her voice rang down the long space.

From the back door came the outline of a large woman, her head wrapped in a *doek*. 'Ma'am?'

'Dora, this is *Mevrou* Zetterling. She's renting Master Fred's house. In Bluegum Street. Please help her with the parcels.'

'Yes'm.'

'And show her *Mevrou* Marie's place. She wants to buy bread.'

'Yes'm.'

'OK. Dora will go with you. If you want she'll help you unpack.'

'Oh. Thank you. That won't be necessary.'

The native woman walked behind her, her broad back erect, the box balanced on her head. She carried the parcelled blanket in her ample arms, and walked evenly along the uneven road, her big broad feet adept between the cracks and stones, her large face expressionless.

Marina carried the bread, a crusty white loaf that was still warm, its yeasty smell teasing her tastebuds.

In another bag eggs, freshly laid that morning…

*

'You're right. She's very thin. And sad. She looks sad,' Annalise reported back to her brother.

*

She sat in the shade of the stoep in the warmth of early afternoon dipping bread into the running yellow of eggs and hungrily chewing crisp bacon and fried tomatoes. From the kitchen came the tantalising smell of perculating coffee and, not able to resist, she left the half-eaten meal to pour a mug of the steaming liquid. She ate and drank and poured a second mugful. Then, comforted by the warm food and drink, she leaned back in her chair and drew deeply on a cigarette.

The veld faced her, flat and colourless, stretching on all sides towards the mountain. Stillness and silence was everywhere and Marina, remembering the city, wondered about the emptiness and endless space.

It was so quiet…so dead quiet…

Suddenly restless, she stood up and walked around the garden. A few shrubs. A patch of gorse. She picked a twig with small elongated leaves from a bush that had pushed through the next door fence and sniffed it. Rosemary. But not what she was used to. The leaves were coarse, the stems tough. It was a wild plant, a survivor in harsh conditions. She rubbed the leaves between her fingers and inhaled the essence. Good for her soup.

She remembered that her brother would be coming the next day. He'd bring her spindle and weaving machine, her sewing machine, her bales of different wools and materials, her cottons and her special pair of scissors.

She would start right away. Store everything in the second bedroom. Work on her trestle table in the light and space of the lounge. Colours and textures, patterns and designs, formed in her mind.

That's what she needed to do. To get into her work again. She'd done nothing for months.

She reminded herself that that was why she was here, in this empty silent place. She'd need to get away. To be undisturbed, quiet and solitary. Her doctor had said, 'You need time. Get away. Somewhere quiet. Be on your own for a while. Find your peace.'

'Find my peace,' she said aloud, wrapping her arms around her thin form. She stared at the emptiness and listened to the silence.

The desolation.

I'll feel better once I start working, she thought, feeling the empty void within her. Once I start, I'm sure I'll feel better about being here.

Light gently entered the house as though not to disturb her. Under the blue blanket she seemed hardly there, the slight moulding of her body, her breathing imperceptible. She'd not stirred from the night before, hour upon hour bestowing her dreamless sleep.

The sun was warming the room when she opened her eyes. She pushed her hair from her face and stared at the huge cupboard. Motionlessly, she waited to be awake in the house in Bluegum Street. She was tempted to turn on her side and close her eyes again. To go back to that unknown place of dreaming or not dreaming.

Then she remembered. Theo was coming today. He was bringing her stuff.

Marina threw off the coverings, her bare feet hardly touching the cold floorboards to the bathroom. She lathered her hair and body. The hot water stung her, reddening her skin. She dressed quickly and wrapped her hair in a turban.

In the kitchen, she struck a match, lit the gas and perculated fresh coffee, boiled an egg and squeezed oranges, surrounded by white walls and tiles trimmed with blue, and worn blue and white chequered linoleum. The sun's rays struck through the wide window and flooded the thickly painted white wooden ledge. She noticed how, even when they were drawn back, the curtains shut out some of the light.

I'll take them down, she thought. I don't need them.

She looked forward to being with her brother. He was younger than her, but seemed the older of the two siblings because, as their mother had said, he had an old head on young shoulders. Another thing she'd said, 'Theo has an old soul…' Marina was not sure what it meant. But she did know that she always felt safe with him.

She heard the lorry before she saw it and ran into the road waving both arms to greet him. 'Theo!' she smiled, hugging him, her face in his chest, his strong arms around her.

'Hi, Marina.' He greeted her with his immaculate smile, his blond hair falling over his forehead. '*Ghott*! What a place! You're in the bladdy *gammadoelis*!'

They laughed, the brother and sister, and looked into each other's eyes, their thoughts and emotions, as always, in harmony.

'I am!' she replied. 'The back of beyond.'

'*Ja*. Feels like off this planet.'

'Well, I needed peace.'

'And you'll have it! For sure! In bucketloads. In this back of beyond.'

They laughed again, arm-in-arm into the house.

'This isn't bad…' Theo walked through the rooms. 'It's clean. And light. And bright.'

'It's fine. Suits my needs. There's a spare room. I'll store my materials there. I can work in the lounge. And the rent's reasonable. Actually quite low.'

'Well, it would be. In a place like this… But,' he added quickly, 'if you're happy, that's all that counts. Sis…' He smiled his enthralling smile. 'Do I smell coffee?'

'You do. And breakfast. Bacon. Eggs. Sausages…'

'No. Thanks. I ate before I came. Just coffee.'

He carried bolts of materials into the house and hauled in a large bale of white cotton. There were boxes of threads, spindles, a spinning wheel, a loom, a sewing machine and knitting needles.

Together they erected the trestle tables.

'I brought you your chairs. To sit on when you work. And your lamp.'

'You're so thoughtful. Thanks.'

'No problem. Just let me know if there's anything else, anything you need. You know. Anything more I can do. Just let me know.'

Marina's eyes filled with tears. She turned away and filled mugs with strong coffee mixed with the cream from the top of the milk.

'You must have some of this bread. I bought it yesterday. It's divine. There's a woman who bakes fresh bread every day. I'll get you some before you leave…

She smeared thick slices with butter and berry jam. Together, they sat on the stoep and looked across the wide flat plateau, pale and hazy in the morning sun. In the distance, the mountains were etched against an immaculate flat sky.

'Have you heard from him?' Theo asked.

Marina jolted back to reality. 'No.' Her voice sounded strained.

'Oh. OK. Just wondered…'

'And you? Have you heard anything from him?'

'No. Not a thing. Zilch.'

They both remained silent.

Marina sighed. She brushed the crumbs from her skirt and took the mugs to the kitchen.

*

She drove with him to Maria's place, bought him loaves of bread, freshly baked biscuits, watermelon preserve and newly laid eggs.

Then stood in the road waving as the lorry bounced its way over boulders and bumped into ruts. Until it was gone from her sight.

Excitedly, she unpacked the boxes and sorted the cloth into colours and designs, the cottons, the satins, the silks, the squares of denim, the odd pieces of felt and the precious velvet. The cupboard became a treasure chest. What could not fit in was stored in open boxes on the floor. There were also skeins of wool, hemp and balls of cotton, a loom, a spinning wheel and a set of spindles. The old Singer sewing machine found its place in the front room.

As she unpacked, images were forming in her mind. A quilt in fiery flames, a sun with spokes in the centre, a tiny woman on a golden spoke.

She looked out of the window at the endless blue sky, the cream and the beige and odd glint of yellow from the gorse in the endless plain, and the browns and greys of the ragged mountains. She stared at the different colours and shapes. Another image formed. Hastily she searched through the shelves and boxes. Yes. They were there. All the colours and textures she would need: aqua and turquoise and royal blue and navy, cream and gold and yellow, ice cream, rich dark chocolate and coffee, pearl grey and smoky grey and charcoal. The distant mountains in velvet. Gentle brown and grey crumpled velvet becoming the layers of that layered range.

She spread her drawing paper and, with a pencil and an eraser, started to draw. Soft lines appeared on the page, lines that would be rubbed out and redrawn many times before she was satisfied. Only then would she mix and apply the paints.

More drafts in paint would be done until she had exactly what she wanted. From the artwork would come her meticulously stitched quilted work.

Her works of art.

She's a perfectionist, said her brother. She's an artist, they said.

Stunning… Unique… Expensive, but worth every penny…

The comments washed over her. Her sense of worth came from creating a piece that came from her heart, from her very being.

A work of perfection, devotion and love.

*

The sun in the west had lost its warmth when she stopped for tea. In her pocket was a crushed packet, emptied of cigarettes. She needed to buy some before the shop closed.

Marina shrugged into her brown coat and walked down Bluegum Street. It was cold. She pulled her collar up and quickened her stride. Already she was learning to sidestep the pitfalls of the broken pavements, the cracks and the rocks.

Annalise had left by the time Marina reached the store, leaving Dora to look after latecomers. She bought cigarettes and a cut pumpkin, its luscious orange flesh freshly beaded with moisture. Tonight was a night for pumpkin soup…

She walked back along the quiet Main Road without seeing anyone. The only people I've met are Frederick, Annalise, Maria and Dora, she mused.

As she sat in front of the fire sipping the steaming soup and chewing bread, the elation of the day drained from her, leaving a feeling of emptiness, a hollowness that had haunted her, that had caused her to run away, to come to this abandoned little corner of the country, a place where she hoped to find her peace.

She lit a cigarette and, unsettled, walked around the room. She thought that it was the curtains, dark maroon, ugly and oppressive. Or the kidney-shaped formica coffee table. Hideous…

Tomorrow those curtains will come down. And that table. I'll either have to cover it or get rid of it. She threw the half burned cigarette into the fireplace and watched its tiny flame being consumed by the fire's flames.

In the distance, the hoot of an owl. A dog barked.

Then – the silence.

*

She was up early the next morning and filled with purpose. Standing on a chair, she unhooked the lounge curtains, carefully folded them and packed them at the top of the yellowwood cupboard.

By the time the sun had reached its zenith, there were white cotton drapes on the windows. By teatime, the formica top was covered with lime and white cotton.

Marina arranged wild rosemary and desert grass in a vase next to a bowl of apples on the sprigged cotton.

In the setting sun, the walls were flooded in a rosy hue. From the fireplace, orange flames burned. Rosemary exuded a sharp clean smell. There was the perfume of apples.

She saw the room in white cotton paling in moonlight, in the flicker of dying embers. It looks better, she thought.

She told herself that she would make covers for the couch and the armchairs. Maroon leatherette. Gloomy. Depressing. Ugly. All that was ugly needed to be covered.

From the window, she saw washing hanging in the garden next door. Sheets, towels, tablecloths. A man's overalls and socks. A blouse…

A woman came out carrying a tin bath, the arms of her jersey pushed up above her elbows, revealing her ample arms. Marina saw that she was broad-shouldered and stocky. She bent from the waist to lay washing on the lawn, then stood up in the morning sun, her face immobile, her hands on her hips.

This is a good opportunity to introduce myself, Marina thought.

'Good morning,' she smiled. 'I'm your new neighbour. Marina Zetterling…'

'*More.*' The woman's face was expressionless, her eyes watchful.

There was silence.

'And you are?'

'Me? I'm Lettie. Du Toit…'

Marina saw her watchfulness, felt her hostility. She continued to smile. 'I see you've done your washing. It's a good day for washing. It should dry quickly.'

'Every day's the same,' the woman replied sullenly. 'Always good for washing.' And then, 'You came Monday?'

'Yes.'

'For how long?'

'I don't know yet. I haven't decided.'

'From Cape Town?'

'Yes.' Marina waited then asked, 'How long have you been here?'

'A long time.'

'Have you always been here?'

'Me? No. I *asso* come from Cape Town. Long time ago.'

'Which part?'

The woman did not answer immediately. Then she said, 'Retreat,' and watched Marina's face, waiting for her response.

Retreat flashed through Marina's mind. Coloured area. Keeping her smile, she said that she'd grown up in the northern suburbs.

'Where?' the woman insisted.

'Parow.'

Verkrampte Afrikaner. One of the Chosen People, the woman thought sardonically. Her eyes were stony.

'So…' Marina was determined to keep the conversation going. 'How come you live here?'

'My husband's from this area. He's a foreman on van Rooyen's farm.'

'Oh…' Marina knew that she was taking a chance in asking more questions. She could annoy this challenging woman. She sensed her aggression, but she desperately wanted the contact. She needed to talk to someone. Anyone. In this lonely place with its empty streets, endless plateaus and endless sky, with its solitariness and silence.

'Do you have children?'

The woman's face seemed to soften. 'A daughter. She's twelve.'

'Where does she go to school? Is there a school anywhere around here?'

'She stays with her grandma. My husband's mother. In Cape Town. She goes to a very good school. A White school.'

Marina pretended not to hear her last comment. 'Well, it's good that she's at a good school, getting a good education. That's so important.'

'She's clever. She always gets prizes. An' she's a good runner. In the athletics team.'

'That's wonderful. You must be very proud of her.'

The woman watched her intently. Her face closed. 'I mus' go,' she said. 'I got work to do. In the house.'

'Yes, of course,' said Marina quickly. 'But I hope that when you have time you'll come and have some tea with me. When you have the time…'

Lettie did not answer. She turned away.

'Bye,' said Marina to the back of her. 'Very nice to meet you,'

The woman nodded. She picked up the tin bath and walked away.

*

'I met my neighbour, Lettie du Toit, this morning.' Marina told Maria among the smells of rising yeast and baking breads.

'Did you?'

'Yes. She was hanging the washing.'

'She's a Coloured, you know.' Maria's kindly eyes glittered. 'Married to one of ours…Du Toit. He works on Fred's farm.'

'She told me about her husband.'

'What did you think of her?' Maria tried to sound nonchalant.

'She seemed, well, a little guarded.'

Maria laughed. '*Ja*. She's very defensive. Well, she did try for White. When she first came. But we saw right away. You can see when they're Coloured…' She looked directly at Marina. 'She tried to make herself the same as us. Tried to act as a White. But we knew. And she knows that we all know. So she's angry. But she must live with it. With her big bluff. What did she think? That we're stupid?' Again that tinkling laugh. This time it sounded ugly.

'It must make her very unhappy,' Marina said tentatively.

'Maybe. But it is what it is. You can't mix oil and water.'

'And her husband? What does he think?'

'Du Toit? He doesn't care. As long as he has a *dop* in him, he doesn't care. Anyway, it's their business.' She put on oven gloves and removed the fragrant browned loaves from the oven. 'They mus' live with it.' She tapped the tins sharply. They sounded hollow. 'All done,' she smiled her warm smile. 'As my mother always said, "To each his own. Each man makes his own bed. He must lie in it." Wait for the bread to cool. Won't take long. Come, let's have coffee…'

*

They sat on the stoep in the steamy fragrance of hot coffee.

'It's getting warmer,' said Maria. 'Another month and spring will be here...'

She seemed kindly. Her shining blackcurrant eyes, her smooth flushed cheeks, her full bosom, her capable arms, her short and sturdy legs were an imbodiment of the goodness that she produced each day.

The warmth of the sun, the creaminess of the coffee, Maria's benevolent presence, her gentle voice, lulled Marina, instilling her with peace.

'Have you always done crafts?'

'I did an arts degree at Michaelis. For quite a long time, I was an artist. I taught, and I painted.'

'Did you sell any of your paintings?'

'Yes. My work was featured in a number of exhibitions and quite a few of my paintings sold.' She went on, 'In fact, I met my husband at my last exhibition.'

Maria glanced surreptitiously at Marina's left hand. No wedding ring. 'Oh. Did you?' her voice was sweet and musical, like a lullaby.

*

Yes. That's where I met him. He was standing there. Head and shoulders above the others in the room. Grey eyes. Sandy hair. A strong face. A strong presence. He was watching me.

I walked towards him. Introduced myself.

'I know who you are,' he said.

'But I don't know you.' I was playful, you could say, a bit flirty. He was, after all, a very attractive guy.

'I'm Hugo. Hugo Renier.'

'The architect?'

'*Ja*. That's me.'

'I know some of your work,' I told him. 'Lovely buildings. The one in Bree Street. And the other in Newlands.'

'How do you know them?'

'I've passed them. I watched the one in Newlands go up. I saw your name on one of the boards...

'How observant of you…' he smiled. His smile could light up a room.

'Do you like my work?' I asked, wanting to engage him.

'I like you' was his response.

I was lost for words.

'Did you hear what I said?' he asked.

'Yes. I did. You said you like me. But you don't know me.'

'I don't have to. I like you. I'd like to get to know you.'

That's how it happened.

Four months later, we were married.

*

Marina suddenly came to herself. God! What was she doing shooting her mouth off about him! Making it all sound so great! Making him sound so marvellous! Hugo! The man that she tried so hard to forget. All those memories that she wanted to obliterate.

'Gosh, Maria.' She swallowed hard. Gathered herself. 'Here I am talking all my rubbish, wasting your precious time. I'm sure you've got lots to do.'

'That's OK. I've got time. I'm never in a hurry,' Maria smiled, leaning forward.

'*Ja*. Well, I'll have to go. Thanks for the coffee.'

Maria watched her leave, the back of her, straight and thin, her ponytail moving in time with her steps. Pity, she thought, rolling dough. I never got the whole story.

In the sharp sunshine she walked, determinedly willing herself to block him. You came here to get away from all that, she told herself. To think of other things. Of good things. Of wholesome things. Not him. Not anything to do with him. What about your wall hanging? Focus on that.

Along the still road, the languid houses and the rutted pavement, she forced herself to think about the wall hanging, the structure, the colours, the shapes. She lit a cigarette, inhaled deeply, and from the stoep absorbed the scene – the beiges and browns, the mauves and purples, the deep azure of the seamless sky, the flashes of olive green, the ochres and dull yellows. The rough and the smooth, the layered textures, the silks and the velvets and the stippled wools, the interplay of fabrics that would come together, replicating nature.

Excited and filled with anticipation, she drew on the cigarette, narrowing her gaze towards what she wanted to convey, the veld and the mountains, the wide flat sky.

Yes. She thought that she now knew what she wanted to do. She needed to select the materials, to pin shapes to the board. She needed to make a start.

*

There were no hours when she worked. Light moved from east to west. It was cold, then warm, and then the air chilled.

Absorbed, enthralled and captivated she pinned and pinned again, changing and changing again, standing back, surveying, then moving forward towards the work, feverishly, creating art out of fabrics. She neither ate nor drank until, finally, exhausted, she stepped into the late afternoon, sipping hot sweet tea.

Silence. Stillness.

The smells of rosemary and lemongrass in the dry air.

In the sky, the sun and the moon on opposite sides of the horizon. The sky blazing in the west. The sky cool in the east.

Amazing, she thought. Night following day. Together in the sky. I should put that in my work. The sun and the moon. The different skies… Yes, she resolved. The sun and the moon. Both will go in.

The veld stretched before her. It reached flatly towards the mountains. Thorn trees, shrubs and clustered bushes lost their shapes. Except for the pale moon, all was grey.

In the featureless landscape, she thought she saw the outline of a man walking towards the mountain. She stared at the image and thought she saw the outline of a dog as his side.

*

Ravenously, she ate sausage and fried tomatoes and beans, wiping the plate clean with bread. She'd waited impatiently for the sausage to cook through, pricking it with a fork and inhaling the mouthwatering smells of beef and pork fat and pungent herbs.

The room was cold. She wrapped herself in the new blanket and sat in the dark at the window watching the sky.

The stars were large and brilliant. They did not seem to be the same stars she'd watched in the city. Those were smaller, not as bright. Here, in this unaltered air, there was nothing to camouflage their luminescence.

The crescent moon was on its course. She stared at it and thought she could see the dark remainder of its shape against an even darker sky.

Silence surrounded her, entered into her. She had no need to stir, no need to reach for her cigarettes.

Outside, an owl hooted, its eyes round and golden. There was the lonely howl of a solitary fox. The surreptitious creeping of an invisible civet.

*

The days came and went swiftly. She rose early and only stepped away from her table when it was too dark to see the intricate work. As always, there were mistakes to be rectified, stitching to unpick, fabrics that needed to be changed. But there was much to be admired about the unfolding wall hanging. The mountain range was the focal point and it was superb in crushed chocolate-brown velvet with violet satin forming shadows.

There was a silver-sequined moon and a brilliant sun in minute stitches of gold thread. There were two skies, one fiery, the other dark, skillfully flowing into each other.

In contrast to the dark mysterious mountain was the empty veld, pale and unobtrusive, except for the tiny outline of a man walking.

She did not know why he was in her work, that tiny image of a tall man. She was not even sure that she'd seen him.

*

She walked into the shadow of Annalise's shop, into her gleaming smile, her glowing eyes, the smooth creaminess of her.

'Oh! Marina!' Annalise greeted her. 'I was coming to find you. To see if you're OK. I haven't seen you for days.'

'I know. I've been working. When I work, I forget about everything else.'

'*Ja.* I was wondering what was going on. I asked Maria if she'd seen you. She said no. Then we thought, but are you all right? I was going to come today. This afternoon. Just to check if everything's OK.'

'Thank you. *Ja.* Everything's OK. But, as I said, I've been working, and now I'm out of everything. I don't have any food. I'm going to have to start from scratch.'

'So you're doing your work,' said Annalise as they walked down the length of the shop. 'I'd love to see your stuff. Maybe buy something.'

'Well, I've only got the piece I'm doing at the moment. But I'll be making lots of different things over the next few weeks. Wall hangings, quilts, cushion covers… If you like, you can have a look before I take them to the market.'

'*Ja.* Please. I'd love that. I really want to see what you do.'

They filled a large cardboard box.

'Marina, next Sunday Fred's having a *braai* at the farm. He said to tell you to come. You'll meet the locals. We're an interesting bunch. Lots of different kinds of people. Will you come?'

'Thank you, Annalise. It's very nice of him to think of me.'

'Well, OK then. I'll pick you up, if you like, at about twelve.' Her lilting voice sang down the aisle. 'Dora…'

Marina asked quickly, 'Annalise, I thought I saw a man the other evening walking in the veld. He was very far away. And it was getting dark so I wasn't sure.'

'Did he have a dog?'

'I think so. As I say, he was very far away.'

'That was Mark.' Her face was turned away. 'He lives on the mountain. Come, Dora. Mrs Zetterling needs you to help her.'

*

'*Mama*,' Dora saw the loom in the second bedroom. 'That thing? Is that to make wool?'

'Yes.'

'Does *Mama* make wool?'

'I do. But I haven't used it for a long time.'

'*Mastah* Fred has wool. In the shed. *Mama* can ask him. Maybe he can give you…'

'Well, maybe I'll ask him.'

'Then,' said Dora quickly, 'maybe I can help to make the wool? If *Mama* will let me? If *Mama* can show me?'

'Would you like to do that?' Marina glanced at the woman whose face was earnestly watching hers.

'*Ja, Mama*! For sure I want to learn. I can help.' Her voice was enthusiastic, her hands together as if in prayer.

'OK, Dora. I'm going there next Sunday. Maybe I'll ask him.' To herself, 'Not for free. I'll buy some if he's willing to sell to me.'

The woman's face was wreathed in smiles. 'Thenks, *Mama*. I will be very heppy.'

Marina decided to cover the wall hanging for a few days. She would then examine it with fresh eyes.

In the meantime, she'd cover the lounge suite, stitching the heavy white cotton, her mood peacefully melding with the still day, the winter sun, the drone of a fat green fly.

Draping the covers over the offending furniture, using sashes to keep them in place, she stood back to admire her work. Much better, she thought. She'd make some scatter cushions in shades of pink and rose. Nice for a change, she thought, to have a pretty room.

Happily, she thought to invite Lettie for tea. To show her. The woman's door opened slightly, suspiciously.

'Hello, Lettie.' Marina's voice was warm. 'How are you?'

'OK.' She was sullen.

'I hope I'm not disturbing you.' Marina hesitated.

Lettie stood solid and silent, her eyes unfriendly.

'I thought, I just thought, that if you had the time you would come and have a cup of tea with me.'

'I'm busy.'

'Well, OK. Maybe another time.' She turned away, disappointed, the door closing behind her.

When she reached the gate, it opened again.

Lettie's voice called, 'OK, I'll come.'

Marina told her that she'd taken down the dark curtains and covered the dark furniture, and how happy she was with the result.

'*Dit lyk goed*,' was the woman's succinct response.

In silence, they sipped their tea.

'I *asso* sew,' Lettie suddenly ventured.

'Oh!' Marina responded warmly. 'What do you sew?'

'I can sew anything. My *ma* was a dressmaker. She made brides' dresses. An' *asso* for the retinue. The bridesmaids. An' the outfits for the mothers. She was very good, an' very busy. Specially for the Jews. She did a lot of Jewish weddings. I used to help her. With the hems an' the linings an' things like that. She taught me beading. I used to help her with the beading. I liked that. She gave me scraps an' left over material. I made bride dresses for my dolls an' *asso* for my friends' dolls. My *ma* said my sewing was very good. She said it was harder to make dolls' dresses because they so small.'

'She's right. Dolls' clothes are very finicky. So, is that what you did? Did you become a dressmaker, like your mom?'

The woman stared at her over her teacup. 'No,' she said deliberately. 'I'm not a dressmaker…' She paused. 'I'm a qualified staff nurse.'

*

Gert had been a motor mechanic who fixed cars in his backyard. He had a reputation of knowing what he was doing, and being reasonable with his prices. He worked on his own, as soon as the sun was up and well into the evenings. His yard was filled with cars and trucks and sometimes a motorcycle.

'Gert's good. Take your car to him. He'll fix it,' they said.

Gert was satisfied. He liked his work and the money was good. One day he would find a wife. Have kids.

Until he had the accident.

Yes, he was a bit drunk. He probably had one *doppie* too much. But it was the other driver's fault. He'd swerved right into Gert. Smashed into the driver's side. Smashed the right side of his body. Left many bones broken. Many nerves damaged.

For months, Gert lay in hospital. He was bolted together with screws. He needed to learn to walk again. His arm hung lifeless.

His only comfort in those long days in hospital was a staff nurse, who, besides taking his blood pressure and dressing his wounds, took the time to talk to him, to comfort him. In her white uniform, she seemed to him like an angel, with gentle hands, a soft voice, understanding eyes.

He saw that she had Coloured blood in her. His people could smell Coloured blood. But he found himself eagerly looking forward to the times she was on duty, the times when she would be at his bedside.

Time passed painstakingly, filling him with hopelessness. She was often beside him, helping him, encouraging him. She also came when she was off duty, in a flowered dress and a string of beads. She brought him chocolate. Told him that she was passing and thought that she'd see how he was.

She wanted to see his blue eyes, the fall of his blond hair, his rare smile.

He wanted her presence, the comfort of her, the feel of her large capable hands.

It was when she took his hand in a different way, and smiled, her warm eyes seeking his, her generous body leaning towards him, that he realised that something had happened between them.

Something more than comfort and friendship. They'd fallen in love.

*

The day came when he was discharged from hospital.

He would never recover the use of his arm and would always walk with a limp. He tried to work with his left hand. He tried employing an assistant. It was no good. His days as a mechanic were over.

They married and lived in Lettie's flat in Retreat. She got him a job sorting and delivering post at the hospital. She fell pregnant and gave birth to a baby girl. He gave up his menial job to care for the child.

He became bored and frustrated. One day, he bumped into his old school friend, Freddie van Rooyen, and told him what had happened to him.

Fred listened. He needed a good man to manage his farms. He knew Gert to be competent, reliable and hardworking. He offered him a job as a foreman on his farm.

Gert accepted.

*

None of this did Lettie tell Marina, who wanted to ask, 'So, how did you come to live here?'

*

She did not talk of her broken heart and tears that streamed down her face when she and Gert left their daughter with his mother. Their blonde, blue-eyed, six-year-old daughter would attend a White school. Their daughter would go as White.

It would need be an English-medium school. Lettie was adamant. She would not have her child brought up as an Afrikaner. Gert's mother agreed, but told herself that the child would only hear Afrikaans in her home. Bad enough that her poor handicapped son was married to a Coloured woman. This girl, this granddaughter would be brought up White, and a proud member of the Afrikaans community.

The Afrikaners. God's chosen people.

*

They drank tea in the fading afternoon. The air was still. The sun moved unobtrusively across the room.

They spoke of Marina's work, of her customers and the markets she attended. They spoke of making jam.

They spoke of the weather. Did it ever rain?

They did not speak of what was in their hearts.

But between the two women and their unspoken words was understanding and quiet acceptance.

When Annalise arrived at the house in Bluegum Street, the mountains were brown against the sky. The sun was riding high, the air motionless, the warmth of spring in the yellow gorse, in the wild grasses.

The farm did not seem far away. They turned off the road and drove through pillars that had, at one time, been imposing. Now they forlornly endured, battered and gorged by clumsy trucks and the horns of bulls. But the fields were fenced and through the mesh were the cattle. A curious cow looked up and gazed at them with gentle eyes.

Annalise managed the steering wheel on the potholed track, her diamonds flashing, her fingernails crimson. After berating Fred many times, instructing him to fix the road, she'd acquainted herself with its pitfalls, and skillfully avoided them.

Teasing wafts from roasts slowly turning on the spit greeted them. *Boerevors* sizzled and rising fat-smoke curled blue. In the shade of a pergola, the guests drank wine and beer, chewed nuts and olives. They'd come from farms and villages, and from the towns, had journeyed long hours and many miles. Travel time did not count in the country. Watching the sun move over a mountain, crossing the stone bridge, passing a cluster of labourers' cottages, someone's brother's farm, and the barn where the skins were dried, all these landmarks were part of the day, becoming a part of the outing.

They clustered, excitedly moving around each other. Rowdy greetings and gusty laughs from the men in their striped shirts, buttons straining over shameless potbellies. Perfumed kisses with bright smiles from the women, rustling in silk, bracelets riding, earrings swinging and pendants nestling warmly between their plump breasts.

There were glimpses of a wheelchair.

'Marina, my wife Laeticia.' Fred stood protectively over her.

Marina saw her warm brown eyes and sweet smile, her delicate face framed by a mass of wavy brown hair, her delicate body in flowered silk.

'Welcome, Marina. I'm pleased to meet you. Fred told me about you. Welcome to our home.' She held out a fragile white hand.

'Thank you. I'm very pleased to meet you.'

'I understand that you do handwork – quilts? That your work is quite beautiful.'

'*Ja.* I do patchwork and other things as well. I've brought you a little gift, something I made.' She handed Leticia a package. 'The wrapping is also made by me.'

The woman drew in a breath. 'Hand-painted wrapping paper. How gorgeous. To go to so much trouble.' She opened the parcel carefully so as not to tear the butterflies. Inside, was a cushion cover painted in the same design. Butterflies dancing around a bush of pincushions.

'This is beautiful,' she breathed. 'Really beautiful. I'll frame the paper and hang it above the cushion. They'll complement each other.' She smiled her lovely smile and looked into Marina's eyes. 'Happy butterflies. They'll make me happy every day. Remind me of you.'

Her husband Fred stood guard, his love a powerful beacon shining over her.

'A riding accident.' Maria informed her. 'The horse tripped and threw her over its head. She was very badly injured. In a coma for months. The doctors never thought she'd survive. Her back was broken in two places. She used to be a champion rider. She's got a lot of awards. Cups and medals and all that. They used to display them. Now they're all gone. Packed away.' Her face assumed solemnity, but, in an instant changed as she smiled broadly to greet Annalise.

They kissed and laughed. Marina waited, awkwardly, but the chatter of the two friends did not include her. She drifted away and found Lettie seated at a table.

'May I join you?' she asked politely, and nodded to the man beside her.

Lettie introduced her to her husband Gert.

'I've just met Laeticia,' she told her. 'She seems a lovely lady.'

'She is.' Lettie did not offer more.

Marina remained quiet. She was learning about her sullen neighbour. If she waited, Lettie would tell her. In her own time. She did not seem to like questions. It was as though every question was probing her personally.

Gert asked how she was settling. Told her if there was anything she needed, they were right next door. She saw his fine eyes, his prominent cheekbones, the suffering he'd endured. She saw their shoulders touch, Lettie's hand on his.

Marina sipped wine and ate a perfectly prepared slice of beef, charred on the outside, pink in the middle. The warmth of the midday sun, the laughter, the voices around her and the sparkling wine filled her with a sense of peace that was foreign to her. She blissfully drifted in this mellowed atmosphere, allowing herself to become steeped in it.

Music brought her to her senses. Tables had been cleared to create a dance floor. The farmworkers jived to the hot music, their dark skins gyrating between the white skins with no one seeming to mind. There was Dora, her sister and her daughter moving in natural rhythm, jiggling their backsides. Fred cavorted with Laeticia, his hands holding onto the arms of her wheelchair, her hands holding his shoulders as he bent towards her, and she laughing with delight as she moved her shoulders to the music. He smiled broadly and stopped for a moment to kiss her. The men roared their approval. The women clapped their hands. In their hearts they marveled at his tenderness towards his wife, this man of granite, stronger than his bull, more vicious than his pitbull. Fred grinned at his guests and bowed.

'He loves her so much,' said Lettie. 'She's his whole life. He'll do anything in the world for her. To help her. He took her to America to see the specialists there. To see if they could help her. He took her to Israel. There was nothing they could do for her. But he keeps looking. I never seen a man who loves a woman like that.'

'How long has she been…you know…?

'About three years.'

She saw Annalise dancing with a tall dark-haired man, her creamy flesh opulent, her blonde hair fluffed, her face prettily flushed. She was moving suggestively under his arm and smiling up at him, her blue eyes shining. He glanced down at her and briefly returned her smile. His face was darkly aquiline, his eyes almost black. He moved gracefully, his broad shoulders erect. Annalise was talking. He seemed to be listening. For a brief moment, he glanced at Marina, and she, catching his eye, immediately looked away.

She thought that he was the man she'd seen crossing the field. Yes. That was him. And there, lying under a table watching him was his huge white dog.

Lettie followed her gaze. 'That's Mark,' she told her. 'And that's his dog, Alabaster.'

Later in the day, she found herself looking out for him, wondering where he was, but he was nowhere to be seen.

In the warm Saturday afternoons, accompanied by lazy flies that stubbornly settled, wasps that flew in and out, and the persistent buzz of bees, the classes evolved.

Dora wanting to spin wool. Frederick gave them a bale. It needed to be cleaned – washed of excess oil and all the burrs removed.

Dora learned to spin – to twist and wind thread from the mass of wool. She wanted different colours. Marina added a pre-mordant to set the dye and Dora watched the yarn boil in simmering yellow onion skins, tea, cabbage leaves, fennel, flowers, black beans and beets. The dyed yarns were set in vinegar and salt. Beautiful colours emerged – reds and purples, greens and yellows, blues, pinks, mauves and delicate rose, drip-drying in the hot sun.

Dora told her sister what she was learning – spinning, dyeing, and now knitting. To make jerseys and pullovers. Then to sell at the market and get in money.

Nombeko became curious. She came.

They sat on the floor with legs stretched out and feet bare. They talked among themselves and laughed aloud, knitting and scratching their woollen heads with the points of knitting needles. They ate bread and jam and drank sweetened tea. They concocted unconventional patterns and knitted in a crazy mix of colours. Marina helped to shape the shoulders and necks of their work. She showed them how to cast off. For the rest, she left them to their own imaginings, to create their own designs.

What emerged were strongly individualised garments, shapeless but intriguing. Eye-catching. Natural fibre, natural dye. In a mix of colours that were distilled from the earth.

They would sell. Of that, Marina had no doubt.

Akhona came to see what Dora was doing at the white woman's on Saturdays, her day off, and why she was going there. Was she working for the white woman? she demanded indignantly. Was she getting money for all this wool stuff? She stood sullenly against the wall watching her mother, watching the spinning wheel, watching the changing hues of the yarns.

She came back again. And again. Her expressions changed from suspicion to intrigue.

*

Akhona wondered into the front room. She stroked the materials, the silks and the velvets. She watched rainbows breaking in the sequins.

She fashioned a bag from calico in the shape of an envelope and closed it with a press stud. She wanted to use the midnight blue velvet to cover the calico. Marina saw the hope in her eyes. Velvet was expensive. She seldom found offcuts. But she could not take the girl's anticipation from her and carefully showed her how to cut the glossy fabric and work the stitching.

The immaculately handmade evening bag, trimmed with sequins, glowed and sparkled. It would fetch a good price at the market.

'Make more,' she encouraged her, but Akhona had lost interest. She wondered off and they did not see her for weeks. Then she returned with ropes she'd fashioned from grasses, and curved stems that she'd scraped and cut into similar lengths.

Marina watched her and waited. The girl sat silently on the floor and played with scraps of cotton. She tacked them together, was not satisfied, unpicked them and started again. Then meticulously and with finite stitches, she created patchwork, lining it with calico. She sewed up the sides, hemmed the edges and threaded the grass rope. She then wound the grass around the stems, fashioning handles.

Her finished work, beach bags in a riot of patterned colour.

The girl then threaded glass beads onto grasses and plaited them, making tie belts.

She made labels by embroidering the letter 'A' onto tape and sewing them onto her goods, not on the inside where they would be hidden, but on the outside where they would be exhibited.

She carefully packed her work into a box and went away. She would come back only once more.

To collect her money.

*

'They naughty,' Dora told Marina as they tidied the rooms in the late dusk of evening. 'The kids. They don' wan' to lissen. Not to the mothers. Not the fathers. They wan' to do their own things. But they don' know. They make mistake and then is big trouble for them. *Asso* for us. The mothers.'

Akhona would not work. 'She's cheeky,' her mother said. 'I hit her but she don' care. She don't help me to clean or cook the food. She wan' to run with the boys. If she pregnant, who mus' pay for the baby? I tol' her. She doesn' want I mus' tell her. She make her face cross an' she go out of the house.'

Her son, her eldest boy, was 'with the politics, with the apartheid business'. He'd gone to Johannesburg years ago. Wanted to be a freedom fighter. She'd received a letter from him a few months after he left and had not heard since. She thought he may be in jail. Or *daed*. Killed by the police. Or the army. They came to the locations and shot them, she told Marina.

Her other son was running with the gangs in Cape Town. He sniffed glue. He smoked *dagga*. He was a bad boy. Stealing and fighting. He came home once and she saw that he had a long jagged scar running down the side of his face. Someone had hit him with a bottle.

Marina listened and shook her head sympathetically. 'And your husband?' she asked timidly.

'My husband is gone a long time. 'I don' see him since the kids was small…'

*

More women came. The workroom, crowded with outstretched legs and bare feet, resounded with the click of Xhosa tongues, with belly laughs, with the clicking of knitting needles, flashes of sewing needles, twists and turns of crochet needles.

Marina carefully labelled the goods and kept records in an exercise book.

Martha: 8 knitted scarves with matching caps – red, green, 2 yellow, 2 white, 2 royal blue @ R10 per set = R80.

Bella: 12 crocheted tea cosies in variegated colours @ R7 per cosy = R84.

Beauty: 9 crochet berets – all in cream @ R9 = R81.

Laleke: 8 prs knitted bedsocks – 4 white, 3 pink, 1 blue.

There were patchwork cushion covers, bags, quilts for prams. Shapeless wondrously concocted knitted jumpers.

Between teaching and guiding, Marina also managed to complete four wall hangings and three large bed quilts.

*

The yellow-wood cupboard bulged.

Annalise thought that Marina needed storage space for all the stuff. Some shelves in the spare room. She would ask Mark, the man who lived on the mountain, to make them.

*

'Dora, I'm going to the market next week. I'd like you to come with me.'

'Firs' mus' ask Mizz Annalise. She can say if I can go. She always need me in the shop.'

'I'll ask her. We'll only be away for a few days.'

She sat on the shaded side of the train facing the changing colours of the earth – the purple gloom of mountain ranges, the flattening of the landscape, a flock of grey sheep, a distant farmhouse – through the grime of the window and the curl of her cigarette smoke.

In the almost empty apartment, she relished the thought of the hours that stretched before her. She'd always loved the movement of trains, the rocking from side to side, the massaging of the seat against her back, the hypnotic click of the wheels on the rails.

She put her feet up and closed her eyes. Immediately, he came to mind. Hugo. Tall. Rangy. With a determined thrust of his hips that enabled him cover ground quickly, making it hard for her to keep pace. His expressive hands. He used his hands when he talked. Unusual for a man to talk with his hands, she thought. But his hands were who he was. He created drawings with them, drawings that manifested in buildings. He was always waving a pencil around, or a ruler.

His hands. How well she remembered the feel of them, their caress. His eyes. His smile.

She felt anguish rise within her, wanting to overwhelm her. She became angry. Don't think about him, she admonished. He's gone. He left you. He didn't want you. Nothing will bring him back. You're wasting time thinking about him.

But he was part of the city that she was moving towards. His buildings could be seen from the market place. His office was down the street.

He left you. He didn't want you. You have to forget him. Forget you ever knew him.

She repeated these thoughts over and over to the rhythmic click of the wheels until her heavy lids closed, shutting down her memories, and her pained face slackened with sleep.

*

Dora clambered down from the crowded compartment at the rear of the train that was permeated with the odour of her people, their honest sweat. She waited for Marina to find her.

They loaded the suitcases onto Theo's van. They would be staying with him. There was a maid's room for Dora in the yard of his house.

*

She preferred the bucket to the shower, filling it with water, vigorously scrubbing her body then pulling on her handmade pinafore in African print and swathing a matching *doek* around her head. She assumed dignity in her traditional garb, her head held high, her back erect.

She looks regal, thought Marina.

They unpacked their goods on their table and displayed the quilts on a stand behind them.

*

The crowds, the voices. The strum of a banjo, the piping of a penny whistle.

The broad smiles of African women selling beaded dolls and necklaces and bracelets. 'And even men's ties made out of beads!' exclaimed an American accent.

The pricing, the arguments, the rude comments in their clicking Xhosa tongue about tourists who bargained them down. Then again the smiles and beads of perspiration on dark brows.

The hippy couple who made shifts from colourful cotton, the smoke from their rolled *dagga* cigarettes floating intoxicatingly in the still air, gazing with glazed eyes, their grubby child with tangled hair playing in the dust…

A thin man wearing eye kohl mincing around his display of painted wooden toys. Arranging them. Rearranging them.

An Afrikaans woman, hair in a bun, round face red, round body encased in a corset, coaxing the crowd, her floury hands offering *melk-terts* and *boerebeskuit*. The labels said cinnamon rusks, sour milk rusks, bran rusks.

The lady with pots of jam.

The craggy sunburned man with potted herbs. The smell of rosemary, of basil. Plaited twines of dried garlic.

An aroma of freshly brewed coffee.

Flowers. Tall irises, gladioli, anenomes and freezias, dahlias, carnations and sweet smelling roses.

American twang, guttural German, subtle French.

Japanese taking photographs with stall holders, photographing beaded dolls.

Smiling

Talking

Looking

Touching

Smiling

*

At the end of each day, Marina counted the money and had Theo lock it in the safe. She meticulously marked what had been sold and what the women had earned. Dora wanted her to keep her share of the profits until they were home. She did not trust this city where people pushed against each other. They can steal the money, she told herself, identifying thieves with her instincts. By the way they walked, the expressions on their faces, the way they hid their hands.

She felt confined by the tall buildings, the narrow streets, the congested pavements. Confused by the traffic lights, the hooting of cars.

She was not used to fried fish and chips.

She longed for chunks of meat, gravy and mealie meal.

She wondered why the black women dressed like the whites, why they did not wear African prints. Why they did their hair in strange styles. *Joh*! She exclaimed to herself. They jus' don' know who they is!

The train was due to leave at two o'clock.

Marina said she was going back to the city. She wanted to do some shopping. Dora was to wait for her at the house. Theo would take them to the station.

She stood in front of the building and stared at the sign that said 'Third Floor – Hugo Renier, Architect'. She went into a bookshop from where there was a clear view of the entrance.

She waited. Stared through the window. The shop assistant watched her and asked a number of times whether she needed any help. Was she looking for any particular book? Was she waiting for someone?

Marina never bothered to answer. She waited to catch sight of a tall man with a rangy walk, with grey eyes and grey-blond hair.

Just seeing him, if only for a few seconds, would have been enough.

ist fogged the mountains, wisps smoking between blue trees. Sun smudges filtered through the smog and made diamonds from dew. There was the early morning call of a thrush and on a high rock the black eagle stretched its wings.

It would be a hot day. When the mist lifted, and the sun struck at beads of moisture on the grasses, steam would build. Snakes would coil, and tortoises pull in their heads. There'd be no sign of the *grysbok*.

By midday, Mark and the meerkats would take to their shelters. But now there were a few hours that would allow him to cut down a tree, to plane logs into shelves and a stump into supports. Three shelves to store Marina's goods. Annalise wanted the work done before Marina returned. She wanted to surprise her.

He showered under the outdoor sprinkler that was linked to a fast-flowing stream, in icy water that flowed down the mountain, his broad back brown and glistening, his dark face thrown back to face the spray. The dog walked around him, wanting the wet on its fur, lapping the pool at its master's feet.

They walked into the forest, the tall man and the big dog, to find a tree that would be suitable.

*

They were not sure how long he'd been there. Someone had reported seeing a man with a saw. Someone else found a half completed log cabin in a glen surrounded by bluegums and violets.

One day, the man came down to the village and they saw that he was tall and strong with dark eyes and coal-black hair, a hawkish nose and a distinct jawline.

He bought oranges and eggs.

They watched him as he crossed the veld in long strides, his dog at his side, and disappeared into the rocks and trees. He'd said that his name was Mark. He told them that he was living on the mountain.

*

He made tables. Circles of tables that could be separated into four segments. Or tables that fitted neatly together, hinged one beneath the other, to be used separately. His mother had had such tables in her house. Placed them in front of her guests, for their cups and saucers, for their plates of savouries and cakes. As a child, he'd moved them apart and put them back together, examining their construction, fascinated by their precision.

He made boxes with lids intricately carved into scenes from the forests, geraniums and proteas, and the animals that were fearless around him. A curious squirrel, a fox, a wide-eyed yellow-eyed feathered owl.

He fashioned small benches and tub chairs, wooden salad bowls, bread boards.

From offcuts he chiselled wooden puzzles for children in all the colours of all the trees that grew in abundance on the mountain.

*

He worked from sunrise to sunset. He worked with sweat on his brow and sweat on his back. He worked his body into long hard muscle. Through heat and rain and wind and sleet. He worked until he was exhausted, until he knew that sleep would come. Deep, dreamless sleep.

But not on the Sabbath. In the deep dusk, he would scrub his body and dress himself in a laundered white shirt and pressed pants. He would brush his hair and don his skull cap. He would light candles.

Then, standing on a rock that faced the plains, in the ancient language of his people, he would call out to his God, ancient words echoing through the valley: *Sh'ma Yis'rael Adonai Elohanu Adonai Echad.*

46

There were other times when his plaintive cry, like that of a wounded animal, would bounce off rocks, the anguished cries of a tortured soul.

They let him be, the people of that insignificant village. They were like that. At first inquisitive, asking questions. Wondering.

Then, somnolence would envelope them and under a resolute sun that arced from the east, and in the air that was heavy and inert, they would shrug. Lose interest. Accept.

Mark became the man who lived on the mountain. The man who worked with wood.

He loaded the shelves onto a trolley, guiding it down the mountain, pulling it across the veld, the muscles in his back straining, the muscles of his arms bulging. He used the strength of his body wisely, with the instincts of a burdened animal. The strain he felt was energising and invigorating, as though he was meant to push and pull, to lift and carry, to bend and stretch.

The mental acumen, the academic prowess, the success and praise and recognition of his past achievements, all that brilliance was in the far distant past.

He entered the house and stood for a few minutes, absorbing the sight and sense of it. The white walls, the cotton covers, the drifting fragrances of potted basil and thyme. Sunlight fell in solid blocks from the bare windows and struck a flame in an oversized pair of steel scissors.

He moved to the second bedroom, the room that Annalise in-structed him to install the storage shelves. Rolls of material stood tall, folded fabrics piled neatly, cardboard boxes packed one upon the other.

It did not take him long to place the long planks of wood on their sturdy supports along the wall. He stood back and examined the work. Yes. It would give her a lot of storage. Should suit her needs.

From his pocket, he took an intricately carved wooden Karoo thrush, no bigger than a thimble, and placed it on the shelf.

The throat of the minute bird was puffed. It was about to burst into song.

Annalise was impatient for Dora to return. Her daughter, Akhona, took her place while she was away.

The girl was sullen. She sat on a box in the back of the shop, her bare feet planted on the floor, her skirt pulled up, elbows on her knees, her surly face in the palms her hands. She was slow to answer. Pretended not to hear. She had no time for the white woman who made her mother unpack cartons, clean the shelves, sweep the shop and deliver groceries, carrying boxes on her head up and down the streets. She scoffed at her mother's salary, said that Annalise's hairstyles cost more in a month than her mother earned in a year. She was dismissive of the Christmas bonus that came each December, two wrapped chickens and a fruit cake, the *bonsella* that her mother gratefully received with both hands.

Her mother shouted at her, told her that they had a house to live in and food to eat. 'How does that happen!' she'd demand. 'From Heaven?' she'd demand. 'From Jesus Christ? No! From the *wek*. If I don' do the *wek*, there is no food. There is no house. Don' tell me your rubbish about the white madam. She pay me aw right. I got enough money for me. For you.'

There were times that Dora would take a stick to her and, with her black eyes rolling and spit in the corners of her mouth, would scream that the girl had to find work, that she would not support her, that she would chase her out of the house.

But Akhona did not want to clean houses. She did not want to wash other people's dirty clothes. She did not want to look after the white children. She hated them, the spoilt white kids! She wanted to go to college.

'What you want!' her mother would shout. 'To dress like the whites! To work in an office! How you do that! You got to know that *wek*. To type on the typewriter! How you learn that!'

On calmer days, her mother advised her to take cleaning jobs and save her money. Then she could go to the city and learn. Then she could 'mebbe *wek* in an office'.

Akhona listened and thought that perhaps she could do that. She cleaned a few houses and earned a few rands. But it all seemed too hard, and, disheartened, she returned to the hut they shared and sulked in a corner.

Yes, indeed. Annalise could not wait for Dora to come back. She wanted to go to the city. She had some business to attend to, some personal business. She fluffed her hair and made plans to go the following week. She booked a long-distance call. To let him know that she was coming.

Dora would look after the shop while she was away.

*

As the train moved from the shackles of the city, Dora's shoulders begin to relax in the congested third-class compartment. She stared out of the window watching the farms rush by, the orchards, the meticulous lines of grapevines, the etched blue mountains and the wide skies. The trip had been daunting for her. The traffic, the crowds, the different tongues, the brashness of her people in their city clothes, in their tan and white shoes, their big jackets and hats perched over one eye. She wondered where her son was. Whether he dressed like these gangsters. Or was he in jail? She hadn't heard from him for a long time. '*Haai*!' she sighed and stared at the floor.

Marina had paid her share of the profits and she was pleased to have the extra money. But she would think again before going back to that place. To that market. Maybe next time she would send Akhona.

She thought that Marina was a good lady. Very polite. Worked hard. Wasn' a madam. Treated them like they was the same as her. Because mebbe she's sad. Something make her very sad. Something happen in her life that make her empty. Mus' be a man.

Not like Annalise. She's a madam. You mus' do everything for her.

But she can be good. If she's happy. When she's cross, she's very rude. Like all the Afrikaners. They think they own the whole country. They can be good but they can be very rude. *Mastah* Frederick, he hit the boys. They tell her that one day they'll catch him! They'll break his head! That's what they say.

She sighed. *Haai*! This South Africa.

The compartment was hot and airless. She let her head drop on her chest and allowed her eyes to close, knowing that her money was tightly rolled and hidden securely between her breasts.

*

Marina again checked the sales in her notebook. She was pleased with the results. Most of the goods had been sold. The women will be happy. They'll come back to the workshop.

She glanced out of the window at the receding city. Thought of Hugo. How much she'd loved him. How she still loved him. She wondered who he was with. A man like that is never without a woman, she told herself.

Sighing, she closed her eyes to the soothing movement of the train and the clicking wheels, allowing herself to move away from that place, from those streets where they walked hand in hand, from the fountain that blew sideways in the south easter, from the spray that they laughingly avoided.

Away from the baby they'd lost. Unconsciously, her arms moved tightly across her belly as though he was still there, the tiny boy that came too soon. Perhaps it would have been better if she had not asked to see him. Had not studied his perfect form or stroked his beautiful face. Had not been left with the image of him. The feel of him.

But she'd wanted that. She'd given birth. Gone through the labour. She'd had a child. She wanted to know that child. Even though he was dead.

It was that image that had haunted her, that made her ill. He, too, had grieved. He'd held her. Cried with her. Was pained and had felt her pain. He offered to pay for a psychiatrist, a psychologist, anyone who could help her. She went. She did everything they told her to do. She even took the pills, against her better judgement, and found herself in a blur, seeing everything through a haze. She'd felt unsteady. Hung onto chairs. Fell asleep during the day. Stared wide-eyed at the black night hoping for the dawn. Had become thin and pale. Listless. Uninterested. Always in a dressing gown…

The train sped across the grey veld. Mountains loomed. The trees were scrubby.

She remembered the house in Bluegum Street. Annalise had promised to order shelves from that man on the mountain. There'd be no charge to Marina, she'd said. It would be a present from her…

*

Annalise was pleased to be going to the city.

He said he was waiting for her. Couldn't wait to see her…

She would have her hair done, with highlights. A manicure. A pedicure. A facial. Perhaps a body massage. They used wonderful oils that made her skin soft and silky.

He was waiting for her.

To take her in his arms. To hold her.

Summer was building in the plateau. It had been a clear blue morning. By midday, the sun caused cows to lower their heads and seek the scant shade of thorn trees. In the oppressive afternoon heat, in the dense air, a storm threatened. From the west, ominous clouds darkened the skies. Lightning crackled, viciously stabbing at the earth, followed by bursts of ferocious thunder.

Then the rain…

Walls of rain crashed down flooding the veld, stopping rabbit holes, overflowing in gutters, viciously splashing on the tops of water tanks, beating on tin roofs and drowning out voices. Flooding the shacks, turning packed floors into mud.

They'd told Marina, 'We don't get much rain. Some years nothing. But sometimes, now and then, a real storm, you know, in summer.'

After the storm, a mild blue day exploding with white daisies and yellow daisies, geraniums, purple violets and burgeoning *vynbos*. Cape thicket and wild rosemary, mountain slopes of pincushions and proteas.

This was the landscape that greeted Marina as she walked along Bluegum Street from the station. The stony terrain she'd left behind was now alive, the rain taking a blank and gravelly canvas and causing it to explode with dashes of bright and vibrant colour.

She watched the stillness and silence of the plateau, the purple range and the broad seemless sky – all infused with peace and calm.

She waited for that peace to come to her.

*

The windows needed to be opened. Air needed to enter.

She moved around swiftly, the rooms filling with outside balm, a bowl of spring wild flowers in a glass jar on the table, the scent of fresh limes in a bowl, the kettle hissing and a pot of fragrant ginger tea.

She walked into the second bedroom, her workroom. There were the shelves stretched solidly along one wall. Ah, wonderful! she thought. That'll give me plenty of extra storage. And enough room for the women to work. She ran a hand along the planed wood. Perfect, she thought. So smooth. Nothing to catch onto the wools.

She found the tiny bird, its minute wings folded, its claws clinging, its rounded throat bursting with unsung song, and her heart filled with wonder. How beautiful it was. How exquisite. He must have left it there for her. She examined it carefully and was astounded at its perfect workmanship. How clever he is, she thought. What a lovely gesture. How kind of him. I must find a place for it.

She tried various places. The minute thrush looked lost on the windowsill and on the coffee table and on the side table next to her bed. No good, she thought. So tiny. It'll get lost.

She went outside and pulled a twig from a tree, secured the bird to the twig and placed it on the kitchen sill.

That's better, she thought. The little bird would be safe there. It could sing in chorus with the kettle.

She decided that she wanted to see him. To thank him.

Mark.

The man who lived on the mountain.

*

She wondered how she would come across him. She'd seen him cross the plateau, a tall figure with a white dog at his heels. He strode purposefully, controlling his orbit. She would not be able to walk towards to him or perhaps call his name. His manner did not allow for casual encounters.

She decided to speak to Annalise. Ask her to arrange for them to meet.

She scrambled eggs, toasted stale bread and took her supper onto the stoep. Air tripped lightly in the mild evening. The sun had set, leaving a pink sky. A paper moon hovered above the range. In the luminous light, moths danced, and from the distance the haunting hoot of an owl.

Then the first stars.

In the darkening sky, the mysterious mountains became ghostly images, holding close their secrets.

*

'It's so hot,' breathed Annalise with a silent whistle and fanning her face with both hands. 'You must come with me to the pool. We can cool off at Fred's place. Have a lovely swim.'

Behind the farmhouse, the pool, surrounded by cement blocks, was squarely set in the ground. They lowered themselves into the cold clean water. Marina swam in long strokes, her hair streaming behind her. Annalise wet herself slowly, delicately splashing water onto her shoulders, fluffing her taffy-coloured hair.

'It's gorgeous,' laughed Marina, pushing back her hair. 'Absolutely gorgeous.' Her face glowed. Her dark eyes sparkled.

She's quite pretty, mused Annalise, sitting on the pool step kicking her feet, her plump thighs spread. If she put on make-up and put a nice colour through her hair she'd look much better. She's got a good figure. A bit thin, but a nice shape.

In the protective shade of the house, they leaned back in chaise longues. Marina closed her eyes. The cool water had washed away her thoughts. Even Hugo, whose tall rangy image came to her every day, was not there. Behind her lids was the colour of brown velvet that drew curtains on her world, indulging her in a peaceful void.

'Marina?' Annalise's voice came from far away. 'Have some lemonade.'

'Oh. Where did that come from?'

'The girl brought it.'

'Thank you. Annalise, I feel bad just coming here, using the pool. Shouldn't we have said hallo to Laeticia? Asked her if she minds.'

'She won't mind. I come here all the time. In any case, she's probably resting. She gets very tired.'

'Poor woman. It must be very hard for them.'

'*Ja*. It hasn't been easy. But that's life. You know, you have to get on with it…what life deals out. Isn't that so?'

'I suppose you're right.'

'Life isn't always fair.' Annalise examined her nails. Twisted her rings. 'I'm sure you've found that out. I mean,' her voice hurried on, 'something must have happened for you to come to this place…'

A silence fell between them.

Then, 'My husband left me.'

Annalise waited.

'I had a stillborn baby. My first. I was devastated. Very depressed. I just couldn't come to terms with the loss. I tried. He also tried. It was hard for him. But it took too long and he eventually walked away from me and from our life together.'

'You still love him?'

'I do. I think about him every day.'

'It must be hard to love a man and then to lose him.'

'It is. Very hard. Sometimes I think I'll never get over him. And yet other times I don't feel that strongly about him. Especially when I'm working.'

'They say that one must give these things time. Time is a great healer.'

'Do you believe that? Others say that true love never dies. And I truly loved him. With my whole heart and soul.'

'I don't know what I believe. I don't think I've ever loved anyone as much as that. Men usually love me more than I love them. That's how its always been with me. Maybe I don't know how to love, as you put it, with my heart and soul. Maybe I don't take love that seriously.'

'I wish I could be more like you. But I'm intense. With everything. My work, my relationships. So when I hurt, I hurt very badly.'

Again they were silent.

Then Marina said softly, 'That's why I came here. To get as far away from the pain as possible.'

They watched the light play on the water. From the field came the lowing of a cow. The drowsy air was filled with sunshine. The women lay back peaceably, companionably, in harmony with the air and the rippling water.

'And you, Annalise,' asked Marina, 'have you been married?'

'Me?' A tinkling laugh. '*Ja*. I've been married.' She laughed again. 'A few times.' Her blue eyes, her red lips, the blush of her cheeks laughed. 'I'm always either married or getting married.'

'They don't last?'

'My marriages? Heavens, no! The longest was four years and that was too long!' Again she laughed. 'I get bored. There's always a better man, a bigger man, a stronger man, a more handsome man. I love men. I get bored and, as they say, I move on.'

'And children? Do you have any?'

There was a shift in the air. The woman with fluffy blonde hair, with dancing eyes and suggestive mouth and rounded breasts and ample hips, with playful hands and crimson-tipped nails, with sparkle and laughter, changed. Became unanimated. Sad.

'I have a son.' She paused, searching for words. 'He's sixteen. A lovely boy. Anthony. The one and only person I really do love. With my heart and soul.'

'A son…' Marina's voice was gentle. 'That's wonderful. To have a son.'

Annalise played with her rings. 'He won't see me.' She turned to Marina. 'It's my fault. I know that. I'm to blame. I was having an affair with a friend of his father. He threw me out of the house.'

Marina was quiet. She waited.

'In the divorce, he got custody. The court allowed me access. I could see Anthony and have him for weekends.' Her voice broke. 'Those were my best times. To have my child with me…'

She turned away. Stared at the water. 'His father hates me. Said that it was bad enough that I was unfaithful, but he detests me even more for sleeping with his friend. Blames me. He's poisoned Anthony's mind against me. Told him that I'm a terrible woman, a whore and a slut who sleeps around.'

She hid her eyes. 'My son won't see me now. Says he wants nothing to do with me. That I'm not his mother. Calls his stepmother his real mother. That breaks my heart. Really breaks my heart.'

She sighed.

Stared at the water without seeing it. For quite a while.

Then pushed herself up and said, 'God, It's hot. I'm going in again.'

She ducked her shoulders under the water. The air filled with her tinkling laugh. 'Come in, Marina,' her voice sang. 'Have another swim. The water's lovely.'

*

'I'm thrilled with the shelves,' Marina told her on the way home. 'They work very well. Thanks so much for organising that for me.'

'No problem. Mark was happy to do the job.'

'But you paid him and I'd like to give you back the money.'

'Not necessary. A gift from me.'

'He also gave me a gift. A tiny carved bird.'

'That was sweet of him. He's a good guy. When you get to know him.'

'You mean, if I get to know him. He seems very private.'

'*Ja*. Mark keeps to himself.'

Annalise told her that he'd arrived some years ago and had moved to the mountain. She believed that he'd been an attorney. Very successful. Then something really bad had happened to him. Something to do with a client. He lost a case. Something happened with his family, but she didn't know the details.

Marina told her that she wanted to meet him. To thank him. He'd done a beautiful job. And also for the little bird. 'Do you think you could arrange that for me?'

Annalise turned to her. 'I'll try.' She smiled. 'I don't know if he'll listen, but I'll try…' She called to the back of Marina's receding figure through the car window, 'He's a Jew, you know. A Jew…'

The man was possessed. He clambered up the rough terrain pushing past branches of trees, his long strong legs stretching over rocks. There was an urgency in his movements, a compulsion to reach upwards, outwards, far away. His hair was awry and his hands flailed. He muttered, his words indecipherable.

The distressed dog followed, struggling to keep up. He whimpered, recognising the madness overwhelming his master, the terrible pain that again was unrelentingly seizing him.

They groped up the steep unforgiving slopes for many hours, the man mumbling incoherently, drenched with perspiration, not caring where he was, or where he was going.

The climb would last for hours, sometimes for days. It would take as long as the pain lasted, ending only when the agony had dissipated, when the desperation and guilt were gone.

The man would collapse in a shaded copse or an exposed clifftop, and lie, unresponsive, in the striking heat of the sun, in the bitter-cold black night.

Then,
consumed and expended
they slowly descended
the man and his dog
hollowed and cleansed

stumble along
from sun into lees
back to the cabin
the cathedral of trees

Dora had come back to a hut that was damp from the storm, the hard-baked mud floor shifting at the front door where the rain had seeped, and streaking whitewash on the walls under the leaking windows. Akhona had half-heartedly attempted to place buckets under the cracks in the roof, but, as her corner of the hut was dry, she did not really care.

Dora went on and on about the wet clothes and the dirty plates but Akhona was not listening. She wanted to hear about the streets of the city, the shops and the buildings. She'd never been. She wanted to go. She wanted to know about her money from the bags she'd made. *How much did she earn?*

She would horde her money with the cleaning money. Go to the city. Learn for a job. Maybe in a factory. To get away from this place. From her corner of the hut. From the shop with that white woman. That Annalise with her loud voice and all her instructions. She would not listen to those orders. She would not obey that white woman.

Dora was angry. Akhona should have covered the clothes with the plastic. Now they smell! She'd have to wash them again. And why she didn' wash the plates? She mus' do it now! Dora was tired. 'Come!' she screamed at the girl. 'Wash this plates!'

She changed into an overall and went to the shop.

'Hello, Dora,' Annalise sighed. 'I'm pleased to have you back.'

Dora waited. She knew what would follow.

'Your daughter's no good. She's very lazy. She was worse than the last time. Doesn't listen to anything. I won't use her again. Next time, you must bring your sister.'

Always the complaints about Akhona. From Annalise. From the other white women. She's lazy. She doesn't listen. She's cheeky. She sulks. Dora wondered about the last complaint. What 'sulks' meant. *Haai*! She sighed to herself. I don' care what they think. My daughter will be

OK. She will go to the city. She will find a job. Earn big money. One day…

*

It was on a warm evening sitting around the brazier eating mealie meal and sucking meatbones that Khwezi appeared. He was thin, seemed taller, his eyes intense but his white smile intact. He sat beside them, the people of the huts, and accepted a bowl of food, pinching the porridge between his fingers and placing it in his mouth. Chewed and smiled. Happy with the greetings he received.

He told them of the underground cell that he'd joined, of the chaos that they worked to create, the strikes and the marches, the demonstrations and whatever else – to upset the government and the business sector. Also the disturbances in the lecture halls at the universities. The burning of Black schools, the burning tyres…

'We will win,' he told Dora. 'We will overthrow the apartheid. We will carry on until we get what we want. We mus' win. We got the numbers. Four to one. We jus' mus' carry on. We mus' never give up.'

Dora watched her older son and sighed. He seemed on fire, his eyes burning in the light of the brazier. She listened to his words but they meant nothing to her. She'd been born into her life. This was all she knew. All the talk of Blacks taking the country. It would make no difference to her.

But she was pleased to be with her elder boy. It had been a very long time since she'd seen him. She wanted to take him in her arms. To hold him again. Of course she would not do that. He would not like to be treated like a child. He was a man. A big man. He was proud.

She was proud of him. 'You will be careful' were her parting words. That, and a parcel of sandwiches and a slab of chocolate.

Akhona walked with him to the station.

'Mama is OK,' he observed.

'Mama is the same.' Akhona told him. 'Every day is the same for her. If that white bitch is OK. If that white bitch is cheeky to her. She doesn' say. For her, it is the same. All day packing and unpacking. Carrying the boxes of groceries on her head to the white people. Up and down. Cleaning the shop. Whatever that white bitch say, she does. When I tell her, she say it's for the money. For the house. That rubbish shack. She call it her house. If I tell her, she shout at me. Tell me to shuddup!'

The whites of Khwezi's eyes became inflamed. His lips formed a hard thin line. 'Does she treat her bad?' he asked in a tight voice.

'She treat all the blacks bad. She an' the others. *Asso* that brother. The farmer. Frederick. He hits the boys with a *sjambok*.'

In the distance was the call of the train. They faced each other. Touched hands.

'Don' worry, Akhona.' Khwezi's face was grim. 'I make a promise. We will get rid of these madams and *mastahs*. We will make it happen. One day. For sure. Our turn will come.'

Before the sun rose and the hoary frost had melted in the desert grasses, before rabbits put their noses out of their holes, and snakes uncoiled, the car drew up at Lettie's house.

The big man knocked rapidly and loudly on the door. 'Lettie!' he exclaimed, his voice sounding gravelly. 'Come quick! Laeticia's very sick.'

The woman heard Frederick's panic, blinked away sleep and instinctively snapped into action. She pulled on a pair of slacks and a sweater, and grabbed her medical bag.

'What's wrong with her?' she asked as the car bounced over potholes in the grim dawn.

'She can't really tell me. She's not with me. She closes her eyes. I think she's unconscious. Then she comes round. Then she goes off again.'

Lettie did a perfunctory examination. Laeticia was not focusing. Her mouth hung open and saliva dribbled.

'She's ill. She needs to go to hospital. There's no time to call an ambulance. We'll have to drive there.'

The farmer hunched over the wheel, put his foot on the accelerator and sped along the national road, overtaking early morning trucks loaded with sheep, his hand on the hooter, swerving onto the wrong side of the road, narrowly avoiding a car coming towards him, ignoring swear words and rude finger signs of the drivers, focusing on the road. Drive drive drive drumming in his head. Get there. Just get there. He thought of Laeticia, his lovely Laeticia. His wife whom he adored. He could not lose her. He drove with his heart in his mouth, sweat running down his forehead, his hands wet on the wheel, his shirt stuck to the back of the seat.

Laeticia…

Lettie sat next to him, her arm over the seat, her hand on the arm of the woman lying in the back with her head propped on three pillows. Her face was drained of colour, her eyes closed. She did not respond when Lettie spoke to her. Only groaned softly. But her breathing was less laboured.

'She seems a little bit more comfortable,' Lettie told the distraught man.

'Watch her,' he responded. 'Don't take your eyes off her.'

*

'It's pneumonia,' Lettie told Marina. 'Frederick stayed with her. I took the night train back.'

She hung the washing, chased the chickens, swept the yard.

Marina saw that her face was wan.

The aroma of freshly brewed coffee drifted across the fence.

'Smells good.'

'Come and join me. I bought it in Cape Town. It's Brazilian.' Marina poured the steaming black liquid into two mugs and added cream and sugar.

'*Lekker.*' Lettie sank into a chair, her slippered feet spread.

They faced each other, comfortably silent.

'Does she often get ill?'

'*Ja*, she does. Always something. She's frail. She gets trouble with her stomach and pains in her back. She's had pneumonia twice.'

'And you look after her?'

'All the time.' She smiled but her eyes were bitter. 'When they need me, they don't see my colour. They very nice. Very 'preciative. But they don't want me at their dinner table. For that, I'm not good enough. The worst is that Annalise. She told me my child is of mixed race. Not pure Afrikaans. She thinks the Afrikaners are God's chosen people. Not the Jews. The Afrikaners. She said she did not like it when the Afrikaners became contaminated. I ask her, I said, "What do you mean?" I was very angry. She just look at me and, cool like a cucumber, she said, "You know what I mean." And then she just laugh. I was so angry I want to hit her. But Gert took me aside and said, "Forget it. Just forget it. She says things she doesn't really mean." The next thing, Annalise comes up and offers me a chocolate. Ah well,' she sighed. 'That's them. But I like Laeticia. She's a lovely lady. I will carry on to help her. Do what I can for her.'

She bit into her biscuit. 'That's life, you know. They rich people, Fred and Laeticia. Can afford anything. Gold and diamonds. They can buy a yacht. Travel the world. But God gave them a burden. A big burden. With all their money, they can do nothing. Go nowhere. Just live out their lives here. Every day. Month after month. Year after year.'

She chewed slowly, swallowed and sipped her coffee. 'They have to stay here. In this godforsaken place.'

The thrush sat on its twig in light that streamed gold and silver through the panes.

Marina saw that the day had not made up its mind. There was sun but there were also clouds. White shapes billowing – a dragon becoming a dog, a sheep with her lamb. Blending… Blurring…

She thought of Mark. Of his coming into her house and placing the boards in the spare bedroom.

She saw him striding through the house carrying the boards, placing them. Then placing his gift of the tiny carved bird.

Did he look at her quilt that was stretched and pinned onto a board? Did he page through her sketchbook?

Was he at all curious about her?

She would have liked to be there. To talk to him.

Throughout the morning he came into her thoughts, the tall stranger from the mountain.

*

She thought that she would walk towards the mountain. To his cabin beneath the trees. Annalise said he did not encourage visitors. Would he be angry if she came?

What should she say?

Just, 'Thank you for the boards and the little bird.' No more than that.

Just, 'Thank you.'

She slipped into slacks and walking shoes, put on her sunhat and dark glasses and crossed the street. There was only the veld between her and the mountain. She'd seen Mark stride effortlessly across the space as though he was gliding on asphalt. She found her steps thwarted by loose stones. Rocks caught her heels. She had to stop herself from stumbling.

She looked towards the mountain. It had seemed nearer than she thought. Now she saw that it was at least an hour's walk, perhaps longer. She went in the direction she had seen Mark take. He crossed the plain at an angle.

She walked on, heat beating down on her shoulders. Around her were boulders. Veld grass pushed up from the arid soil.

She heard a rustle behind a bush and shuddered.

She stopped to wipe her forehead. Under her hat, her hair hung in damp tendrils. Her shirt was wet with perspiration. She should have brought water, she thought. She was not prepared for this long hike. Had not realised how far the mountains were, how rough the terrain.

She looked behind her. Her house had disappeared behind a ridge. She estimated that she was about halfway there.

The sun shafted through the clouds.

Her head ached. Her legs automatically moved forward. She did not want to stop but could not carry on. She sat on a rock and rolled her aching shoulders. Perspiration streamed down her face. Her body was damp with sweat.

Around her were bushes of wild flowers born in the gasping dryness of the place, surviving in the wind and the heat, and cold black nights. Rocky outcrops, shrubs and scrubby thorn trees. The mountains loomed ahead, sun-blackened and forbidding.

Again a rustle in the grass. A porcupine quivered, its sharp quills extended. She shivered uneasily despite the heat.

She should not have come. She decided that she would not go further.

*

The sun was sinking in the west when she reached her gate.

She sank into a chair on the stoep. Her watch showed that she'd been walking for hours. She stared at the place she'd come from, remembering how enchanting it seemed on the day she returned from the city. How she'd been captivated by the vibrant splash of daisy colours paletting the grey and lifeless plain.

When you're there, she thought, in the midst of it, in the heat and dust of it, you don't see that beauty. You become concerned with finding your way through rocks and stones. You focus on putting one foot in front of the other. You watch out for snakes and spiders.

You don't see the daisies and wild violets. You don't see silver sunbeams breaking through the clouds or hear the song of a Karoo lark.

You're alert to the rustle of something in the grasses. Wait for the hiss of a snake. Shrink from the darting tail of a green lizard.

You look to the mountain as you stumble over the rough terrain. To the mountain that that is home to Mark, forbidding, aloof, removed and remote.

Far far away…

*

She stepped out of the shower into clean underwear and a loose cotton dress. Her skin was rosy from warm water, her hair damp, her face naked. As she sprayed a scent of roses onto her neck and wrists, there was a sharp knock on the door. Barefoot, she faced the man who filled the space with his height and broad shoulders. She could not see his eyes under his leather hat, but his face suggested a smile.

'Mark,' she gasped. 'Oh. Hi. I…I've just come out of a shower… Haven't put my shoes on yet…' Awkwardly, she caught her hair. 'Please. Come in.'

'Annalise said you wanted to see me.' He made no move to enter.

'Yes, I do. I wanted to thank you for the shelves. They're perfect. They work really well. Just the right size. Hold a lot of stuff. I really like them.' She was aware that she was gabbling. She told herself to stop.

But she carried on. 'And the little bird. Thank you for the little bird. It's exquisite! I love it. So tiny. So beautifully carved. Such wonderful detail. Please. Come inside.'

'Thanks. I won't. I'm on my way back.' He pushed his hat to the back of his head.

She could see his deeply set eyes, dark and clear, with fine lines formed from harsh sunlight. Not laughter. He didn't look as though he laughed much.

Then, 'I saw you yesterday.'

'Did you? Where?'

'In the veld.'

Startled, she asked, 'Where were you?'

'On the mountain. I saw you coming across the veld. Then I saw you turn back.'

'Oh. Yes. I did go for a walk.'

'You walked quite a distance. In that heat.'

She looked into his eyes. 'I was coming to you,' she answered softly, 'to thank you for your work.'

He was silent.

'Would you have been angry if I'd just turned up?' Her voice became a whisper.

'Angry?' He paused. 'No. Not angry. Surprised, maybe. But not angry.'

*

She watched him through the window, through the yellow sun strokes, his dog Alabaster at his side, gliding across the landscape in long strides. He disappeared and she recalled that the ground went in waves. She waited. Perhaps she would see him again, his tall lonely figure in the mirage of waves that flowed towards the purple mountain.

*

The days drained colour, leaving places and faces beige. Dogs panted and drooled and fell asleep in the hot shade. Bees were quiet. Birds still. Leaves did not stir. The air would not move.

But the evenings were beautiful. As the sun began to set and the skies flamed, as the moon became a beacon lighting the mountains in shivering silver, stars danced, and perfumes of basil and rosemary floated.

She sat in the silver evening in the flowing essences and pervasive peace. She thought that she would invite a few people for drinks. Make some snacks.

Better than that, she could could have a dinner party. They've all been so kind to her.

That's what she would do: invite them for dinner. All of them.

And Mark.

*

Excitedly, she drew up lists of people drinks food. And candles. She'd make candles. Lots of them…in different colours…different shapes… to light up the garden…

The stars were her inspiration. She decorated her handmade invitations with glitter.

You are invited to my Glitter Dinner
Please wear glitter
In your hair, on your clothes, on your shoes

The evening was bright with stars. The moon, a chandelier in the sky, beamed white light onto the crevassed surfaces of the mountains, silvered the veld, and cast its opalescent glow into the shadows of the garden.

The air was heavy with the aroma of roasting pork stuffed with wild herbs and the pungent whiff of spiced cocktail sausages. From the barbecue came the cranking sound of slowly turning meat and the hiss of fat on burning coals.

Many candles burned, tall and pink, squat and yellow, infusing glimmer into the glitter, revealing rainbows in sequinned hair, on spangled wrists and decorated bosoms.

The men had also obliged. Frederick pinned a twinkling brooch to his Stetson. Martinus wore a rope of tinsel from the Christmas tree decorations box. Gert brought a box of sparklers that sparked figure eights in the moonlit garden, complemented with laughter and guffaws, with effervescent wine and the exploding foam of beer.

Dora came round with another tray of drinks. She was there to serve. To collect plates and glasses. To clean the mess after the guests had gone. She'd willingly agreed. The extra money would be useful for her.

Annalise took a glass from the tray. 'Good evening, Dora,' she greeted the black woman in the apron. 'Thanks. I'll have another drink.' Her eyes narrowed. 'Don't work too hard. I want you wide awake at the shop tomorrow.' Then, seeing the twisted tinsel around the black woman's throat, said, 'Can you beat that! Even Dora's wearing glitter…' and laughed spitefully.

From a turntable, Frankie Laine, that singing cowboy from other plains, other stretches of veld, other ranges of mountains, belted out 'Rawhide'.

> Move 'em on, head 'em up
> Head 'em up, move 'em on
> Move 'em on, head 'em up, rawhide,
> Cut 'em out, ride 'em in…

In the jewelled sky, the pearl moon, the diamond stars, in the opalescence and the glitter, the ghost dog bounded across the veld, its sharp nose quivering in anticipation of the odours of *braaied boerevors* and roasted pig that teased the desert air, ignoring its master's voice.

'Hey! Alabaster! Wait!' He was a tall dark shadow in the crowd. Taller than the men there. He greeted Marina with a casual wave of his hand. From a distance.

She went towards him. The shadows of smiles between them were broken by the wide pearl smile and dancing blue eyes of Annalise, who came between them and took his arm, brushing her soft breast against him.

She's flirting with him, thought Marina. What does she want with him? I thought she had a man. Goes to the city to be with him. What does she want with Mark?

Maria seemed to read her mind. 'Annalise loves the men,' she smiled. 'And, she added conspiratorially, 'they all love her.'

It was true that few men could resist her. She had the right amount of plumpness and smoothness, soft blonde curls that fluffed about her pretty face, expressive eyes that danced or could become grey, a slow intriguing red-lipped smile that revealed glistening pearl teeth. Her expressive hands, tipped in crimson and highlighted with diamonds, were used in soothing and suggestive ways, ways that could make a man shiver with excitement. Her curved hips. Full thighs. Well shaped carves and smooth white feet. She was someone they wanted to touch, to hold, to kiss.

She had this effect on men. She knew her attributes. She used them to her full advantage. This was her payback. Her revenge on the world. She would not allow anything to get in her way. She did not care who was hurt in the process.

She danced with him. Held him close to her. Only one dance. Then Marina saw him disengage and walk away. Away from Annalise. Away from her. Away from the party.

*

Marina could not sleep. The noise of the party, the laughter and the chatter and the music, would not leave her. Restlessly, she padded around the house barefoot, made herself tea, lit a cigarette, and, from the stoep, watched the moon recede and the stars fade.

She watched the first timorous grey fingers of dawn creep over the mountain and merge with the motionless, featureless landscape. She surrendered to the peace without thought or feeling while in her lap the tea turned cold and grey ash dropped from her cigarette.

The sun, moving west, had struck all the rooms by the time she woke. Her head throbbed and her eyes were slits against the gleam of white walls. She stood up, held onto the bedpost and pushed her hair away from her moist pale face. 'God, I feel terrible,' she mumbled. Her mouth felt like straw. She should not have drunk the red wine.

She stumbled to the bathroom. The water drenched her hair and rushed down her body. She turned her face up and waited for the saturating spray to clear her head, to make her eyes hurt less.

It had been a great success, the Glitter Party. Everyone ate and drank hugely, laughed and danced, and left in the early hours of the morning calling loud goodbyes and 'thanks for a lovely evening'. Dora had been marvellous, washing the dishes and glasses, packing the empties, sweeping the house and stoep.

She's a good woman, thought Marina. And then she thought, she knows how to handle herself. No one speaks to her. They just give her orders. But in spite of their off-hand treatment, she handles herself with pride. She has dignity. Something in her is intact. Something that other people can't get to. Honestly, the way Annalise sometimes talks to her… The way she shouts at her. Dora's face closes up and her eyelids come down. But she seems to hold herself together. Just carries on.

That Annalise… She's something else.

And what about Mark. She's all over him. And she's supposed to have a boyfriend.

*

Annalise rang the doorbell. 'Brought you a lovely roasted chicken,' her voice sang. 'I was sure you didn't want to go near the kitchen after all that cooking yesterday.'

'Oh. Thanks. That's very nice of you. Come in. I've just brewed fresh coffee. To be honest, I only got up a little while ago. With a helluva headache! I drank too much wine. Coffee helps.'

They sat in the fading day, in the reflection of pink cloud-light, in the tender movement of air, in the delicious coffee aroma.

'It was a lovely party.'

'Yes. It went off well. I'm really pleased.' There was a pause. Then, 'Mark disappeared quite quickly.'

'Well, that's Mark. A bit unpredictable.'

'I hardly spoke to him. When I looked for him, he was gone.'

Again silence.

'I saw you had a dance with him.'

Annalise examined her fingernails and turned her rings. 'You have to understand Mark. He doesn't mix well with people. And if he feels uncomfortable, he leaves. Without saying goodbye. He just goes.'

'I've noticed that.' Then, 'You seem to understand him. He seems comfortable with you"

Annalise lifted her chin. 'We know each other. I do understand him and we are comfortable together.'

Marina could not hold back. 'I hope you don't mind my asking but, when you see him, you act as if you kind of, well, as if you fancy him. If you know what I mean...'

'I find him attractive. I mean, he's a gorgeous guy. Don't you think? Any woman's fancy.' She paused. 'You probably fancy him too...' Her eyes narrowed. 'Don't you?'

Marina refused to be trapped. But she was resolute. 'You say you find him attractive. But I've heard that you have another man in your life. Someone you're seriously involved with?'

'I do. I have a lover in Cape Town.' She turned her pretty glittering smile to Marina. 'We're mad about each other. In fact, I'm going with him to a conference in Paris next week. But that doesn't mean that I don't also fancy Mark. Or, for that matter, any other guy who may come along...'

'I don't understand. I mean, how many men can you fancy at once?

And what about the man in Cape Town? Does he know that you…
um…like to flirt? I mean, that you find other guys attractive?'

'I don't know if he does or he doesn't. I really don't care. That's how I
am. I like men. They like me. I don't take these things too seriously.' Again
that tinsel laugh.

Then, conspiratorially, 'My lover left his wife for me.'

'So you don't mind breaking marriages…'

'Agh! I don't go around breaking marriages. Men fall for me. They're
unhappy with their wives. They want me. They say I bring sunshine
into their lives. I mean, if a woman doesn't know how to keep her man
happy, that her fault, don't you think?'

'No. I don't think that. Sometimes there are circumstances that create great sadness in a woman, that make it very difficult for a woman
to come right, and that can cause a problem in a marriage. So, no, I
don't think it's always the fault of a woman if she can't make her husband happy. I think the couple should be given the time to work things
through.'

Annalise turned her full attention to Marina. 'My dear,' her tone
was deprecating, 'if you think that men hang around wanting to work
things through with their wives, you're sadly mistaken. Men are different creatures. They're looking for lightness, brightness, a pretty face, a
soft body. They're really not interested in psychological crap like working things through. If they don't get that glow from their wives, they'll
find it somewhere else. Because, my Marina, there are always women
out there willing to be what men are searching for.'

'Women like you…?'

'If you like, yes. Women like me. Women who make them feel
good. Turn them on. Give them what they need.'

Marina asked, 'What about the intellect? The meeting of minds?'

'Well, no one likes to be in the company of a fool. But brains? Marina, I have seen a university professor in the company of a woman with
a PhD, deep in conversation. Completely engrossed. Then a young girl
walks past, pretty, sexy, and the professor forgets everything that he was

talking about. All his attention is now on the girl. I think, more than brains, a woman needs to know how to listen, how to respond. To reach out with a smile, a soft touch. A bit of tenderness. That's what a man needs.'

Above them, the sky was dark. The stars seemed remote.

Over the mountain, an eagle circled.

Marina watched her walk away, her blonde hair silver in the night light, her supple shoulders, the gentle sway of her curved hips. She turned at the gate, sending Marina the glimpse of a smile and a half-wave of her hand, and in that moment Marina saw what she'd meant about being a woman.

*

She lifted her thick brown hair with both hands, then let it fall, straight and dull, to her shoulders. She explored her face with her hands. Felt the bones. Saw the dark shadows below her eyes and in her hollow cheeks. Met her brown lusterless gaze. Touched her pale lips.

She stood in front of the mirror and examined her thin body – small breasts, narrow hips, thin thighs. She turned sideways. Hardly any bum.

No wonder he lost interest in me, she thought. It wasn't just the sadness and the awful depression that enveloped me.

It was all of me. Not just my intellect. He didn't really care about my abilities. He wanted me as a woman.

I failed him. I'm plain. Unattractive. Unappealing. That's why I lost him.

She cried. She cried for the loss of Hugo, for the loss of her baby, for her dead marriage. She cried for the lost years, for the time when she was young and fresh and beautiful.

For she had been beautiful. But she'd not cherished her beauty. She'd neglected the gift that she'd been given. Allowed her beauty to fade. Became brown and jaded.

She woke the next morning, and reached for her cigarettes. She remembered how her smoking used to upset Hugo. He said that she smelled of nicotine. Her mouth, her hair, her skin, her clothes. He said that she should give it up.

Perhaps she should… At least try…

*

The cool shower, the brisk towel, the free-flowing cotton dress, her hair in a loose bun. It was a good start to the day. Again she wanted a cigarette. 'Don't,' she said. 'Try not to. It's nine o'clock. See if you can get to ten…'

There was a lot to do. She'd planned a series of sequential wall quilts that would be framed. The first – the face and flowing orange hair of a woman, her hands seeking. The second – a man with black hair under a checked cap, facing in the direction of the woman, his hand up to greet her. The third – the two figures intertwined.

Her artistry came into full bloom with her capacity to convey the yearning of the cloth images for each other in the first two pieces, and the joy of their ultimate union in the third.

'She's remarkable,' they said. 'Imagine conveying expressions and emotions using scraps of material…'

'A real artist…'

'So talented…'

*

She persisted. Minute by minute, hour by hour, then day by day.

She dreamed cigarettes, woke to find herself moving her hand to her mouth, fingers poised as if holding a lighted cigarette, drawing on the imaginary weed. Her craving for nicotine was overwhelming.

Lettie du Toit told her it was the hardest of all addictions to break, including cocaine. 'The cigarette companies upped the nicotine content, to make sure that people got properly hooked,' she said.

Marina craved. Cakes and chocolates. Ice cream. Foods she'd never eaten. The richer, the sweeter, the better. Foods crammed with sugar seemed to help, if only for a short while.

One evening, so overwhelmed was she with craving that she begged Gert du Toit for a cigarette. Frantically she drew on it.

The bitter taste surprised her. She inhaled again then squashed it under her heel.

*

The class had dwindled. Dora and her sister Nombeko continued to come. Lettie joined them from time to time, sewing dolls' clothes and knitting tiny pullovers and leggings. They sat, this disparate group, often in companionable silence, working, drinking tea, becoming drowsy in the summer heat.

Ahkona had lost interest. She was difficult and rebellious, but she had a plan in mind. She would go with Marina to the city instead of her mother.

She would not come back. Find work. Even housework, if she had to. Or in a factory.

Get away from this terrible place. Never come back.

*

Marina was not smoking. She felt that she had lost something precious. The friendly cigarette that had greeted her each morning, the smoky haze that surrounded her in the late evenings, was gone.

She knew, at the same time, that she'd done the right thing.

Her sallowness began to fade. Her skin was clearer, her eyes brighter, her hair more lustrous. Her face was warmly tinged with sun-gifted hues, her breasts fuller, her body softer.

There was no longer the irritating cough that she'd woken with each day. The nervous energy that she'd lived with, the churning in her stomach, the increased beats of her heart – had dissipated. Her vigour became more wholesome, and at the end of the day she was able to fall into fitful sleep.

'You look marvellous!' from Annalise. Then, with a narrowing of her eyes, 'What have you done? You look a different person.'

*

Frederick brought her two kittens.

She was delighted.

'*Agh wat*!' he exclaimed. 'You don't have to thank me so much. We were going to drown them. Then Laeticia heard. She said, "Don't do that. Give them to Marina."'

She went to the city with flesh on her bones and a healthy bloom in her face. Her eyes glowed. Her hair was lustrous. She resolved to have it cut and shaped. Perhaps some highlights.

She would buy a dress. Something sophisticated to show her new curves. High-heeled shoes to compliment her shapely carves. Hugo always said that she had good legs. Pity no one saw them, he'd said. Always hidden under those long skirts.

She'd buy perfume. Have her nails done. Maybe a facial.

She'd do all these things and then she would contact Hugo. Have coffee with him. Let him see the new 'her'.

*

Akhona came with her. She was helpful and obedient. Contrary to her usual sulky moods, she smiled often. Marina noticed her white teeth, her flawless coffee-coloured skin, her straight shoulders, her long neck, the elegant turn of her head. Her unspoiled hands, her long slim fingers.

She's beautiful, Marina thought, wondering at the change in her behaviour. She's probably excited to be in the city. Her first visit.

'Stay close to me, Akhona,' she instructed. 'I don't want to lose you.'

The market days passed quickly and successfully, with almost all of their goods sold. They would go back at the end of the week.

Akhona was told to wait for her at her brother's house. She should rest, said Marina. She gave her some magazines.

'I've got a few things to do. I won't be very long. Wait for me.'

*

She saw him through the window, the shape of his head, his shoulders. Her heart began to beating fast. Her hands felt clammy.

Hugo…

She walked towards him, her hair fashionably bobbed, her eyes made-up, her lips rosy, in a fitted cream suit and court shoes.

Eyes followed the alluring movements of her body to the table, where the tall man rose to greet her. He took her hands in his and, smiling broadly, they kissed, a man and a woman who were pleased to see each other.

'You look amazing!' he exclaimed.

'Thank you,' she smiled. 'You also look very well.'

'Thanks. So you're in the country. The fresh air certainly agrees with you. Are you working?'

'Yes. More than ever.' She told him about the group of women who had joined her to learn to weave and knit. 'It's wonderful to see how motivated they are. They pick up things really quickly and they're making so many different things.' Marina laughed. 'They sit on the floor with bare feet, talking and laughing. I love it when they come. They make everything seem happy.'

'You seem happy, Marina. I'm very pleased to see that.'

She looked into his eyes. 'Seeing you makes me happy, Hugo. You have no idea how much I've missed you.' She reached across the table to take his hand.

He leaned back in his chair. His expression changed. 'I've met someone,' he said quietly.

She waited, her hands tightly clasped.

'A lovely woman.'

She heard him say that they'd been together for a few months. That he'd fallen in love with this woman. That he wanted to marry her.

Marina's heart froze. She tried to tell him that she was happy for him. She wanted to say she wished him well.

The words would not come.

They sat for a while, trying to reach each other again.

She thought she heard him say that he had just come back from overseas.

He noticed that she was not smoking.

He asked after her brother.

They tried.

Then, through a blur, she saw him stand up, heard him say that he was pleased to see her again, that she should keep well, that he wished her everything of the very best. She felt his hand momentarily on her shoulder.

Then he was gone.

*

She arrived at her brother's house.

Akhona was not there. She'd left a note in carefully structured letters.

> I say goodbye Mizz Marina. I not coming back with you. I stay here. You tell my mother I will find *wek*. She mussen worry for me. I will come and see her. Thenks for this message to my mother. Goodbye from Akhona.

*

Marina could not think of Akhona.

Her make-up was streaked, her suit stained.

She'd cried on the bus and had not cared who noticed.

She saw the dog pushing through the gate, its keen brown eyes, its inquisitive nose, its tongue hanging. It had run ahead of its owner, a handsome animal with thick white fur, huge paws and an impressive expressive tail. An animated feline, spirited, stimulated, looked after and loved. A dog who loved back intently, with awareness, attention and loyalty.

Always running ahead. Watching for anything that might threaten its master. Menacing growls, sharp fangs, powerful jaws.

Alabaster.

Behind the dog, Mark.

The man who seemed carved from the mountain. A giant rock of a man. Powerful, armoured, with muscles of granite.

They were a team, the man and the dog.

Their eyes pierced and penetrated the plateau, the forbidding mountains, the endless skies. Their ears tuned in to the whispering grass. They were prepared for wild creatures and treacherous cliffs.

They survived. They belonged.

The man and the dog.

*

Her eyes and smile glowed as she showed him the shelves filled with patchwork and embroidery, with crocheted caps, with quilts and cushion covers, with knitted pullovers.

She chatted about her work and the women who came, what they made, and told of the market where she sold her goods.

She showed him the tiny lark on a twig on the thick white wooden windowsill that waited to sing together with the singing kettle.

She made a pot of tea.

He accepted a slice of fruit cake. He ate a second slice.

She spoke, her sentences running into each other, hoping to keep him there. He did not interrupt. He listened intently, his eyes not leaving her face.

He ran his finger over a quilt that was pinned to a board. She saw that Mark did not fit into the house.

He was awkward on the cotton-covered couch. He preferred to stand, leaning against her work table, his long legs crossed.

Alabaster, too, was big for the space. He sat on haunches, focused on the kittens, refusing the water in the bowl.

It's time to go, the dog commanded.

'You should come to my place. See where I live,' were Mark's words as he strode to the gate.

'I'd like that,' she replied.

She thought that there might have been the glimpse of a smile.

No. Perhaps not. He was not a man who smiled.

*

She moved through the rooms that had been filled with his attentive silence. He'd left behind an energy and the image of his powerful presence.

There was much to know about this man. Much hidden in his silence. She wanted him to talk to her. She wanted to know what he thought.

Of the people who lived here, he was the only one who could challenge her mind. But he was not a man to be rushed. She would have to wait.

Marina walked each evening in the *dorpie*, up one street, down another, rough ground beneath her feet, sidestepping cracks and potholes, dry air against her face.

There were those who lifted a friendly hand. Some called, '*Goeie naand, Mevrou.*'

'Others greeted her with 'Hello. *Hoe gaan dit?*'

She was known as the woman who made '*aantreklike goede*' – 'pretty things…'

The mood of the place had settled on her. The soulless streets. The lifeless houses. The people who lived there but did not make themselves known.

The nothingness of it.

From the west, a mild breeze wafted.

The only sound the persistent chirp of a cricket.

She walked carefully, watching for cracks in the broken pavements, seeing resolute weeds push up between them. Lizards escaped into their holes and a field mouse tiptoed delicately across a street.

Nothing seemed threatened in this nothingness. Marina was blending, becoming one with the void.

It's a peaceful space to be in, she thought. Living in a vacuum where life merely exists. Night follows day. The seasons pass. The months, the years.

How strange, she thought, that I have managed to make something of this godforsaken place. That being here is doing good.

*

There was a bristle in the air.

Marina was not sure if it was actual or imagined as she opened the door to Annalise, her blonde curls fluffed, her crimson smile, her pearl-wet teeth.

'Hello!' She burst into the room in her swinging bottle-green coat, flushed and excited, her heels sharply clicking the wooden floor. 'I'm back!' Her laugh tinkled. 'From Paris! From the City of Love.' She hugged Marina and held her arms, attempting to waltz her around the room, navigating the table and the couch.

Marina laughed with her. 'And did you find love?'

'Did I find love?' Her laughter sprinkled through the air. 'Let us say, love found me!' She threw off her coat and collapsed in a chair, her legs crossed, her shoe dropping off her heel. 'Love! Head-over-heels love! Honestly, I've had many men, but this one is really something! He couldn't let go of me. Not for a second. And spoilt me. Bought me clothes and perfumes. Jewellery.' A bracelet moved up and down her wrist. 'Was even looking at diamonds, but I said not yet, too soon. I'm not ready to commit.' Again her lovely laugh. 'I'm having too much fun.'

'Do you mean he wants to get engaged?"

'Of course, darling. They all want to get engaged. I've got so many diamond rings, I don't know what to do with them. Another diamond ring? Not right now.'

She sat up and rummaged in her bag. 'I brought you something…'

The silk scarf folded exquisitely around Marina's shoulders, fluctuating colours as she moved this way and that.

'*Pragtig*,' breathed the woman in the chair. '*Baie pragtig*,' and sighed with satisfaction. 'I told my boyfriend that this would suit you. I was right. It's perfect.' She sighed again. 'Oh Marina, I had the most wonderful holiday. Paris is just amazing. The shops, the shows… And the people… Smart. Chic. Now I know what they mean when they say the Parisians are chic. And the food… Divine! Just thinking about it makes me want to go back.'

Then she became practical, remembering where she was. 'So how have things been here?'

'OK.' Marina smiled at her friend's rude awakening. 'This is not Paris, as you know. Everything's the same as when you left. No news really.'

'Not surprising. Nothing ever happens here.' The dancing lights in Annalise's eyes turned to glitter. 'And Mark? Have you seen him?'

'Ja. I did. He came by for a little while.'

'Only a little while?' Her voice was mildly curious.

Marina nodded. She wondered again about Annalise. This glowing woman who seemed satisfied but also seemed to want more.

'Well,' she exclaimed. 'I must go. See what happened in the shop while I was away.'

'OK. Thanks for coming by. And thanks again for the beautiful scarf. I really love it. You chose well.'

Annalise laughed. 'To tell the real truth, I never chose it,' she said. 'My boyfriend did. He chose one for me as well.'

Again it was Alabaster who ran ahead, who pushed open the gate, who barked at the door. Behind him, Mark, his eyes hidden under a broad-brimmed hat, the muscles in his arms shining.

'Are you busy this weekend?' he asked.

'No. Not really… I mean,– I always have things to do, but nothing urgent…' Her words ran away with her.

'Would you like to come to my place?'

'Do you mean now? Today?'

'Yes. If you like.'

She thought quickly. That long walk in the heat. The long walk back. Would she manage?

He was outlined in sunshine. She wanted to be with him. To see where he lived. How he lived…

'You can sleep over, if you like,' he said, reading her thoughts. 'I have a spare bed.' There was a rare smile. 'I assure you that you'll be quite safe. If you stay over, you won't be doing the walk twice in one day.'

Her heart quickened with apprehension. Sleep over? In a log cabin on an unknown mountain with a man she did not know…

But I trust him, she thought.

'OK,' she smiled. 'That should be quite an adventure, sleeping in your cabin. I'll just throw a few things in a bag.'

He told her that he would lead the way. She should place her feet in his footsteps. His fluid strides were reassuring. She followed the effortless movement of his agile body.

He does seem to glide, she thought.

They reached the edge of the plateau and began the ascent of the mountain along a natural path of flattened grass through coppices that were interspersed with clumps of pink pincushions and exotic orange birds of paradise.

Then the trees.

A cathedral.

Vaulting bluegums filtering green light, walls of yellow-wood, ground stained purple with violets and orange with geraniums. A tree trunk thickly coiled with ivy – a Solomonic column – spiralling majestically to the roof-dome of this nature-church.

An aura of reverence.

A sanctuary of perfect peace.

He looked down at her from his imposing height and said, 'Can you feel it?'

'Yes.' Her voice was small in the vaulted space. 'It feels…holy.'

He nodded. 'Awesome.'

'Overwhelming…'

'In a beautiful way…'

'If I believed in God, I would say that I feel God's presence.'

'You don't believe in God?'

'No.' She thought of her dead son. 'I stopped believing…'

He did not ask why.

Alabaster ran ahead and barked.

'Let's carry on,' he said. 'We have a little way to go.'

In a clearing shaded by a canopy of trees was the log cabin, red and blond, with a door secured with strong hinges, and a framed window.

The room, warm and stale with captured air, was spacious, with board floors and well caulked log walls. A ledge held mugs and plates, pots, a frying pan, a stone jug and a coffee pot. Another ledge held books. In front of the window a wooden table and two three-legged stools. An old coal stove in the centre of the room. Along one wall a bed of wooden slats with a thin mattress. A similar bed stacked sideways near the door. From its slats hung Mark's clothes.

It was simple and sparse, but reassuringly filled with Mark's presence.

'You've done a great job,' Marina told him. 'Everything fits together. Feels cosy. Safe. Secure.'

'Thanks.'

Then, 'Have you ever tasted wild jasmine tea?' He lit the stove. Filled the kettle. 'With honey?'

'I don't think so.'

'Try it. Tell me what you think.'

*

In the blackness above her, she could see the huge stars – Orion, The Three Sisters, The Bear. Trees stood guard around the clearing.

In the distance, the howl of a wolf. An invisible owl hooted, its eyes gold coins. Alabaster, ears laid back, rose now and then, prowled and sniffed.

From the pot, the tantalising aroma of wild rabbit stew cooked with yams that Mark had dug from the forest floor, flavoured with wild profusions of herbs, dowsed with red wine.

'Absolutely delicious!' Marina exclaimed. 'I was starving! You're a good cook. And everything from the mountain…'

'Of course. It's all around you. You just have to look for it.' He smiled his rare smile. 'I've got another treat for you…'

Wild strawberries, tiny and sweet, and rich goats' cheese.

She sighed with satisfaction. 'That was a gourmet meal, Mark. Fit for a king.'

She was aware that they'd eaten in silence but it had not felt strange. Like the animals, she thought. Masticating. Swallowing.

He warmed water from the stream and filled a tin bath. 'Have a wash and get into your pyjamas. Give me a shout when you're finished and we'll get your bed ready.'

She fell asleep almost immediately, filled with warmth and comfort, feeling safe and protected. Like being in a womb.

*

He'd showered and dressed by the time she opened her eyes to sunbeams striking the gold-brown logs. A solid block of sun flung across the floor

and the air filled with the song of a lark. She stood in the doorway holding her hair away from her face, her feet bare on the bare floor.

Smoke rose from a fire. Mark crouched and pushed in another log.
It smelled of the forest, of pine needles.

He glanced up. 'Hi. Did you sleep well?'

'Like a log! What time is it?'

'Well after nine.'

'Nine! Why didn't you wake me?'

'Why would I? You were sleeping so peacefully.'

'I had the best sleep ever. No dreams. I don't think I even turned
over.'

'It's the mountain. It does that. Would you like to have a shower?
The water comes from the stream. I can rig it up for you.'

'Yes. Please.'

'I must warn you – it's cold. Really cold.'

'Jesus!' she yelled. Cold? It was freezing! It took her breath away.
She gasped.

'Try and stick it out.'

She thought she heard him laugh.

'You'll feel great afterwards.'

The icy water was clear and clean and pure. She opened her mouth.
She'd never tasted water like that. Standing in a stream of drenched sun
stripes filled her with joy and song. Her spirit danced.

She's beautiful, he thought as they dipped bread into egg yolks, eating without speaking.

After extinguishing the fire and brushing the cinders, she followed
him through the forest. Onwards and upwards. To a clifftop.

'You can see everything from here.' His arm swept across the ex-
panse. 'The veld. The *dorpie*. Frederick's farm. The roof of your house.'

It lay below her, a giant patchwork, perfectly textured. stretching
to the horizon. More beautiful than anything she'd ever made.

God's patchwork, she thought. And thought, it's a long time since
I used the word 'God'.

In the rose flush of evening, still wrapped in the bliss of the mountain, she looked towards the place where she thought the log cabin nestled.

She thought of Mark.

She recalled that although they had spent time together, they'd hardly spoken. She told herself that there'd been no need. They'd been comfortable in their silence.

In that silence, they learned about each other.

She was thinking about Mark as she walked towards the sharp knocking on her door.

Mark from the mountain. Mark of the mountain. Craggy impenetrable rock. Craggy impenetrable Mark.

You can get to know the mountain, she mused. You walk its paths, smell its scents, taste its fruits, listen to its sighs.

In the same way, you get to know a person.

With these thoughts, she opened the door to the serious squat figure of Lettie.

'What is it?' Marina asked, concerned.

'Laeticia's dead.' The woman's voice was flat, her chin low, her strong shoulders slumped.

'What!'

'She's dead.'

'What happened? How did it happen?'

'I just come back from there. From the farm. The driver came to fetch me. When I got there, she was cold. She had no pulse. I could see right 'way she was dead.' Her hands shook.

Marina guided her to a chair.

'Frederick told me when he went to her this morning she was lying so still and white. He tried to wake her. He called her name. He said he tapped her on the shoulder. Then he said he could see she wasn't breathing. He tried to sit her up. He hit her on the back. To try and get her to breathe. Poor man. He didn' know what to do. He started to scream. That's what the driver told me. He ran through the house screaming, "Get the doctor!" That's what he was screaming. "She's not breathing. *Alle Hemel*! Get the doctor! She needs help! Quickly. *Asseblief*!" So Johannes came to fetch me. When I came, I could see. She was gone.'

Lettie paused. Took a deep breath… 'She must of die in the night.

Already there was rigor mortis, you know, stiffness in the hands. I try to tell him. I try to say that she's gone. But he was like a mad man. Jus' walking around like in circles and screaming. Screaming her name. Screaming to get a doctor. Banging his head with his hands. Running to her. Then running out of the room. I told Johannes – he's the driver – to go to get a doctor from the hospital. To see Laeticia. To tell Fred.'

'How terrible,' Marina murmured. 'Such a lovely lady.'

She thought of that haze of flowery perfume. The cloud of hair around her delicate face. Her pale and perfect skin. She recalled her clear gaze, her smile, her hands. How she used her hands to punctuate her words. Her gentle voice. The way she saw more than others. The way she understood.

How she was loved. By everyone.

'Lettie,' Marina was filled with sadness at the loss of a woman she hardly knew – a woman as delicate and fragile as a beautiful butterfly, 'what do you think happened? '

'Looks like she had a heart attack. Maybe a stroke, I don' know. They sleep in separate rooms, her and Fred. She couldn' have called out. If she did, he would've heard. He always listens out for her. The slightest thing, he comes. She's his whole life. Looks like that she died in her sleep.' Her hands twisted. Her shoulders humped.

She blew her nose and sighed deeply.

*

The funeral took place at the farm under a grove of almond trees that Laeticia had planted as a young bride. Everyone said they wouldn't last in the dry desert air, but, except for one sapling, they not only lasted, they thrived. She would pick the nuts from their branches, peal back the husks and dry the kernels in the sun. She would make almond tarts.

Now, in the flimsy shade of this grove of nut trees, she was to be laid to rest.

Everyone from the district came, and from far away. Farmers in stiff black suits and collars that were tight around their red necks, women in black, some with veils over their eyes, children solemnly dressed in their church clothes.

In the relentless heat of the day, in the beating down of the sun, they stood, a sombre group, as the minister read from the Bible and said the eulogy, as the coffin was lowered, as those nearest to the grave threw flowers.

As the first clod of earth resounded, a sound that was not human, a great and tortured cry rang out over the vast fields. Fred bent over the grave, his head in his hands, his body racked with suffering.

Accompanying the terrible sobs of the big farmer in the black suit, came a great keening from the groups of black workers, and an agonised wailing.

A choir of anguish reached to the heavens, and echoed in the far-away hills.

*

They moved slowly over the patched and sandy field. There was the sad low mooing of a cow. On the horizon, the black dots of distant birds. The sun on their black-clad shoulders as they moved in silence to the farmhouse.

They shuffled past the front parlour where Laeticia had lain in her white coffin, perfect in peaceful death. Frederick, gaunt and unshaven, his massive shoulders slumped, his hair awry, received their words of comfort without hearing them, moving his shaggy head from side to side like an animal in great pain. His brother came to him, leading his shambling body from the crowd to the study.

He sank into his swivelling leather chair with sunken eyes, uncomprehending, disbelieving.

*

Laeticia had told Marina, 'I grew up on a farm. When I was little, I saw the film *Red Shoes*. I decided there and then that I wanted to be a ballerina. There were no teachers, no ballet school, and so I made my own ballet steps, my own movements, dressed in a tutu that I'd sewn by hand. I had no ballet shoes, so, barefoot, I made my own dances. I used to dance around our swimming pool, little jumps and twirls, moving my arms in the air, with my hair in a bun. I was in my own world. Deliriously happy. I believed that I would one day be the greatest ballet dancer in the world. That was my dream.'

Marina recalled her musical laugh, the ballet-like movements of her hands as she spoke.

'Of course, I would never be a ballet dancer. I became far more interested in my horses.'

Marina recalled her sigh.

'My beautiful, beautiful horses. They were the most important of all in my life.'

Marina had asked her how she'd met Frederick.

'At a local dance. He came all the way across the hall to ask me. To be honest,' she'd smiled her radiant smile, 'he couldn't dance to save his life. He had on big leather boots and he had very big feet. They kept getting in the way. He was so embarrassed. He kept apologising. But he would not let go of me. So we stumbled around the dance floor as best we could. He was a hopeless dancer but I liked his face. He had eyes as blue as the sky. And I liked the feel of his arm around me, I liked the feel of my hand in his. He has huge hands, you know, but gentle. With me, his hands are always gentle.'

She'd told Marina something else, in absolute confidence. Said that she did not know why she was telling her, but that she trusted her. She trusted that she would not tell anyone. 'We couldn't have children.' She'd said that it wasn't her. That she was OK. Healthy. It was Fred. He couldn't make children. He'd told her that he'd had measles when he was twelve or thirteen. 'At puberty, you know.' That left him with a very low sperm count. Almost nothing. She said in a whisper, 'My big strong husband is sterile.'

Mark was outside in the shade of the broad stoep, Alabaster at his feet. He looked unlike his usual self in a dark suit and a collar and tie, his thick hair brushed back.

She smiled. 'You look different. Like a business man. Or a lawyer.'

'How did you guess?'

'Guess what?'

'That I'm a lawyer.'

'I wasn't guessing. It just came out. I could just as easily have said a doctor, or an accountant. So, you're a lawyer?'

'No. I *was* a lawyer. I'm no longer a lawyer.' His black eyes looked away.

She realised that she had inadvertently stumbled into his past, a past that he kept hidden, that he did not want to remember.

'Very sad about Laeticia,' she murmured. But he had turned away from her.

Annalise came towards them, her face pale, her eyes mysterious under her short black veil. 'Hello,' she said, kissing Marina.

She slipped her arm through Mark's, moved close to him, and with a sad smile said, 'I'm pleased you came.'

Together they moved to the far end of the stoep.

Marina saw that she was murmuring to him, and that he was listening intently.

*

She glanced at the wall of books and remembered…

On the side table was *The Magic Mountain*. Also *Sons and Lovers*.

'I love my books.' Laeticia had followed her gaze. Her perfect skin was suffused with pleasure.

'My mother,' she'd smiled. 'She was from England. Never fitted into farm life. She tried but it was not for her. So she lost herself in reading. The only times she was really happy, excited, was when a parcel of books arrived from overseas. I inherited her library. It meant very little to me until after my accident. Then I discovered the world of books, and these books have become my salvation. They are my friends. Like my mother, they comfort me. Bring me joy.'

Frederick was in the study. He spoke to Laeticia as though she was in her chair at the window, the light playing in her hair.

He told her of the funeral, of those who came, and what the pastor had said about her. Her beauty, within and without. Her gentleness and her compassion. He told her how the pastor had described her love for everyone, and that everyone, even the farm workers, had loved her. He spoke of those farm workers who ululated and wept. Of the psalms they sang from where they stood on a hillock, separate, but refusing be separated from her.

Laeticia, the white woman they loved.

His wondering thoughts recalled her saying only a few days before she died, his Laeticia who never spoke ill of anyone, 'Fred. I'm sorry to say this, but I think that your sister Annalise is not a good woman.'

*

Fred remembered Laeticia's words. Annalise is not a good woman.

Annalise… The youngest of the brood. The prettiest. The most indulged.

More than pretty. Plump and pink. 'Like a pearl,' his father used to say. 'She reminds me of a perfect pearl.'

From a baby, she was in his arms, on his lap, on his horse, in his car, in their bed. Laughing and bouncing around on her baby feet. Demanding. Petulant. Getting her way.

With her father.

With the men in her life.

She was resented by her brothers and sisters. Only Frederick, the eldest boy and older than her by sixteen years, was intrigued with her antics and entranced by her curls, the rosy blush of her skin and her pretty dimples.

She should have grown into a pampered, happy young woman, but something had spoiled her. Something troubling deep inside her.

People said she'd spent too much time with her father, that he was too fond of her. That it was not natural for a father to be like that with his daughter. 'Who knows what he's up to?' they'd darkly whispered.

She knew, but she chose not to remember.

The damage had been done.

She was not sure that the fault lay entirely with her father. She'd indulged him. She might have been born with those wiles…

*

Frederick thought about Annalise. Was she a bad woman?

*

She'd made a good marriage to a good man. She'd destroyed that marriage. She'd destroyed the relationship with her son.

She'd destroyed the men in her life who had loved her, who'd wanted her for a wife.

She was rude to the Black people. They hated her.

Maria had told Laeticia that Annalise was a nasty and selfish woman. 'But please don't tell that I said that,' she'd begged.

There was the other side to her.

When she'd hurt their feelings, she would make up for her spite by bringing food or buying gifts. She won them over relating stories of the outside world. London. Paris. With glowing eyes and shining red lips, with pearly teeth and expressive plump white hands, with diamonds and satins, she would tell, and they, captivated, would listen to her musical voice, her tinkling laugh.

The women wanted her company.

As for the men… Well, she was almost forty, and they were still salivating.

All these thoughts circled in his head.

Then Laeticia's words echoed. and Frederick thought, maybe she was right. Frederick thought, my sister is not a good woman.

They watched Frederick shrink within himself. His broad farmer shoulders folded inwards. His strong back humped.

The hair on his head whitened and stiffened in unruly tufts. The hair on his face bristled.

His meaty hands, previously like cleavers, that had pulled an ox and beaten a boy, became smaller, defenceless.

There were spots on his shirts. His trousers were creased. He walked with an untied shoelace.

He'd lost his Laeticia.

They shook their heads and said that it was as if he had lost his own life. Was a walking corpse. Unkempt. Hollow.

'We need to do something,' Annalise determined. Cheer him up. After all, life must go on. He wasn't an old man. He could still enjoy himself. Find another woman. Go overseas.

Yes, she told herself. He needs to get over her. Get a new life.

I mean, she said to herself. She was in a wheelchair. What kind of life was that for him? OK, she rationalised, he did love her. We all knew that. But after all, he's a man. He needs a woman. A whole woman. All men do.

She thought excitedly, we'll have a *braai*. With music. It's well over a year since she died. Surely he won't object to a little music. Maybe a dance or two. What's the harm in that? And we'll invite everyone. All the single women.

Who knows? Maybe he'll take a fancy to one of them.

*

They sat around the table on the terrace. Stars glimmered and the moon was a great orb in velvet black skies.

They tried to be happy. To tell jokes. To laugh.

They ate blackened meat and oozing boerewors. They drank brandy. Opened another cask of wine. But moths flying into the lights cast grey shadows.

Fred said to Marina, ' Come with me. I want to show you something,' and she followed his sad and shambling figure down the dark passage to Laeticia's bedroom.

He pointed to the butterfly-covered cushion, to the framed hand-painted butterfly wrapping paper. 'She loved that,' he mumbled. 'She used to stroke the cushion. She used to look at the butterflies on the wall. "Marina gave me that," she used to tell me.'

*

Annalise was drunk.

Her lipstick was smudged, her blonde curls tangled, her eyes bleary. She took off her shoes and swayed unsteadily to the music. Her hands, sparkling with diamonds waved about. Bracelets rode her plump arms.

Lettie thought that she would fall. She took the inebriated woman by the arm. 'Careful, Annalise, you can trip, hurt yourself.'

Annalise shook her arm free. 'Don't you touch me,' she hissed. 'I'm enjoying myself. Don't spoil my fun.'

'Sorry.' Lettie shrugged and sat down.

'Sorry? Sorry!' A poisonous glint shone from Annalise's eyes. 'You should be sorry. A Coloured woman sitting at our table. With us Afrikaans people. The people of this land.'

'Annalise!' Gert protested, protectively placing his arm around his wife's shoulder. 'Don't say that! Lettie's a fine person.'

'A fine person?' sneered Annalise, hands on hips. She leaned towards him. 'You mean, a fine Coloured person. Sitting here as if she belongs. As if she's a big madam.'

'Stop it, Annie,' reprimanded Frederick, his voice hardly audible.

Lettie's face turned grey. She moved away from the table. Took her bag. 'Come, Gert.' Her voice trembled. 'Let's go.'

'That's right! You go! You have no place here.' Annalise's eyes filled with hate. 'You must watch yourselves, you two! I'll report your daughter to the authorities. To the headmaster. A Coloured girl at a White school. She shouldn't be there. She has no right to be there, I'm going to report her!' she screeched.

Her vile words pierced like knives, venomously echoing around their receding figures.

*

'I'll kill her,' the woman's body trembled violently. 'If she tries to do any harm to our child, I swear I'll kill her. I'll strangle her!'

Her voice was strangely muted, her face carved in dark stone. 'I swear by my God I'll kill her.'

Her eyes stared without focusing. Her breathing was labored.

'If she does anything bad for our child, I swear I'll choke her until she dies. With my own hands.'

Gert watched her. He was afraid.

This was not the woman he knew. This stranger was a woman possessed.

Marina had marinated chicken breasts, had peeled and sliced luscious orange pumpkin and opened a tin of peas. She poured wine and cream over brown pears and baked them with prunes. She chilled a bottle of Chardonnay and placed a bowl of mixed nuts next to a bowl of oranges.

The late afternoon was bathed in cold beige light. She lit the fire, placed the chicken and vegetables in the oven, and luxuriated in the comfort of a hot bath.

Mark was coming to dinner. She was excited to see him again. He made Hugo seem less important.

She thought of Hugo with his piercing flint-blue eyes, his sandy hair falling over his brow, who, in her dreams, turns away from her and in long agile strides disappears around an unknown corner or over an alien hill. In some dreams, she runs after him, desperately striving to catch up with him. In other nightmares, she's anchored to the spot, her legs leaden. Only her voice calls, Hugo… Hugo…

She remembered how he changed from being her loving and concerned husband to someone whose eyes became less intense, whose smile was less engaging, becoming more distant with each passing day.

Until the day he declared that their marriage was over. He had met someone else.

She needed to brush those memories away.

She briskly rubbed herself until the blood rushed to her skin. She dressed in a flowery skirt and a white woollen sweater and tied the French scarf around her shoulders. She brushed her hair until chestnut lights gleamed, outlined her dark eyes with kohl, highlighted her cheekbones and painted her lips with coral lipstick.

She was surprised and pleased to see how pretty she looked, her reflection glowing back at her. The tantalising wafts of cooking food and the scent of pine resin from the burning logs mingled with her perfume.

In the grey dusk the room was rosy in the flicker of flames. Hearing the pattering of paws up the path, she told herself, Mark's here. It's time to open the wine.

*

He preferred to stretch his long body on the rug near the fire, Alabaster at his back watching the cats.

They sipped wine and ate, and spoke of the time that had passed.

'You look amazing,' he told her. 'So different from when you came.'

'How different?' she teased, flirting with him. Mark made her feel girlish and pretty.

'Well, you look healthy. And younger. And happy. You look happy.'

She wanted to say, 'Being with you makes me happy.' But she held back those words and answered, 'I am happy. And I feel do healthy. And contented. This place agrees with me.'

'Yes, I know what you mean,' he replied. 'There are no demands here. No expectations. No interferences.

'One has a chance to breathe. To do one's own thing.

'To move at one's own pace.

'To be alone.'

*

He closed his eyes to the crackle of the fire, to the steady breathing of the sleeping dog. 'I was married.' His voice was quiet. 'I have children. Two girls.'

Light from the flames played on their shadowed faces.

He lay on his back, hands behind his head, looking at nothing. 'I may still be married. I don't know. I don't know if she divorced me...' His words drifted.

He rolled over to face Marina, his eyes now focused. 'I was a criminal lawyer. I was known to be good.' He paused then said, 'One of the best.'

107

They waited silently for his thoughts to become words.

'I defended criminals. Got them off. I got paid. Very well paid. I made a lot of money.' He looked away. 'My wife could have whatever she wanted. And the kids. We had a beautiful home. Smart cars. Overseas trips. The works.'

The room was silent.

Then, 'She wasn't happy. My wife. She didn't like what I was doing. The guys I was defending. She said they were dangerous. Mafia. Cutthroats. Murderers. She wanted me to go into some other aspect of law. Something more civilised, she said. I told her no. I was making a fortune. In just a few years, I'd become a rich man. I had a name in the city for winning. I was winning cases but, more important, I was winning big time for myself, and for her, and also the kids. I had a big ego. I liked where I was and I liked what I was getting out of it. It was like I was living on the edge, rubbing shoulders with all those scumbags. Exciting. Exhilarating. But she was very unhappy. She said she was worried about the kids. That she felt unsafe. I told her she was crazy. Why was she worried? Nothing would happen to her or the kids. I was a lawyer. That's what lawyers did. They defended people. That was my job, for God's sake.'

He became silent. Marina waited.

His voice dropped, his words directed to the flames as though he wanted them consumed. 'I lost a case. A big one. Very unusual for me. I was not in the habit of losing cases. The guy, my client, got life. At best twenty-five years without parole, with good behaviour. It was bad. His family were devastated. I'd promised to get him off. That's how conceited I was. So sure of myself that I guaranteed them I'd get him off.'

He rolled over to face her. 'I said we'd appeal. Took a lot more money from them. But we lost the appeal. We were lucky the judge didn't increase the sentence.'

Mark's eyes became black and seemed to sink into their sockets. His lips were a thin hard line. 'The guy's family blamed me. They said I fought a crap case. They told me I wouldn't get away with it! What I'd done to their brother, their son.

She thought that there were tears in his eyes. But she couldn't say for sure.

'They came to my house in the middle of the day. She'd just fetched the girls from school. They raped her. There were three of them. They all raped her. That was bad. Terrible. But the worst part is,' his voice faltered, 'the worst part of this story is that they made my daughters watch. Eight and six. That's all they were. They made them watch. My kids. They made them stand there and watch as they ravaged their mother.'

She wanted to take his hand but he moved away. Rose abruptly to his feet and called the dog.

*

She watched him walk out of the gate. He seemed broken.

Her heart went out to him. What a terrible story. Their lives shattered. Their family destroyed. His career destroyed. No wonder he's a wreck.

She washed the dishes, her thoughts swarming. So that's how he turned up here. He ran away. Poor guy.

She wanted to reach out to him. To comfort him. To hold him. To try to take away some of the pain. But he won't let me.

And yet, she mused as she washed the dishes, Annalise seems to be able to talk to him. She seems to be able to get through to him. To talk to him. To take his arm. She seems to be able to do it.

*

She woke with the unfurling of fingers of wan light and walked to the lounge to open the windows to clean cold air. In the last vestiges of night, the plateau and mountains merged shapelessly into the sky. The stars were gone, the moon just a whisper. In a corner of the lounge, the cats who hunted lizards and small birds in the dark were now tightly curled into their basket, taking each other's warmth.

She watched the silent expressionless scene. Immediately she thought of Mark and how much she wanted to be with him – in this grey dawn before the sun came, before the moon was gone.

*

In the blank canvas before her, the figure of a tall man was striding towards the mountain.

'It's him!' Her heart beat against her palm.

She watched him disappear, his dog smudged against his side. 'I thought he went back last night. He must have stayed over.'

But where?'

She did not have to ask.

She knew.

*

A car had parked in the street, the driver unsure of the house. There were no numbers. They'd faded or fallen over the years.

He'd needed to see her. He needed to hold her suppliant body in his arms, to kiss her luscious mouth. His lovely fiancée. On impulse, he'd hastily dressed and driven fast and surely along the deserted roads, arriving at the village earlier than he expected.

He waited in the fading darkness for the sun to rise.

A large white dog walked to a gate, lifted its big head, sniffed the air and gave a short sharp bark, sensing something. A man followed, pushing his arms through the sleeves of his thick duffel coat. A woman came out and took his face in her hands. They kissed, drew apart and them came together again, her body melting into his. Her blonde curls were entangled in his hands, her hands in his dark hair. In the silence, he knew her laugh. They walked to the gate, her arm through his, the tall man and the soft shape of the blonde woman in a flowered gown. Again he saw them kiss.

He watched the man turn, abruptly, striding away, the dog gambolling ahead of him. He turned at the end of the road and raised his

110

hand. She raised her fingers to her lips and blew a kiss at his receding figure. Then she gathered her gown around her and walked barefoot into her house.

*

Annalise was in the shop. There were shadows beneath her eyes and her carefully preserved face sagged. She covered her mouth to hide a yawn. 'Marina. You're my first customer.'

'Am I?'

'*Ja*. So, what do you need?'

'Nothing. I don't need anything.'

'So why are you here?' Annalise's smile was not in her eyes.

'I've come to ask you something.'

They watched each other carefully.

'Well, what is it?'

'I need to ask if Mark stayed over at your house last night.' Marina's words fell over each other. 'He had dinner with me. Left at about nine. I thought he would go back to his cabin. But then I saw him early this morning. Walking towards the mountain.'

'Mark?' Annalise shrugged. '*Ja*. He did stay at my place last night.'

'Oh.' Marina's voice was small. 'Has he done that before?'

'He has.' Then, defiantly, 'Why do you ask?'

'Do you have a spare room?'

'A spare room?' Annalise laughed. 'Oh, Marina. Honestly. You are so naïve. No, I don't have a spare room. I have a big warm double bed.'

'So Mark sleeps in your bed?'

'Well, what do you think?' The woman's eyes glittered.

'But you have a boyfriend. Someone who wants to marry you. How can you sleep with someone else?'

'Do you really want me to answer that?' The woman sounded bored. 'I sleep with whoever I like.' She combed her crimson-tipped fingers through her hair.

That's when Marina saw the ring. 'Where did you get that?'

'This?' Marina's plump thumb fingered the sapphire. 'From my fiancé. This is my engagement ring. Beautiful, isn't it?'

*

Marina stumbled into the blinding light. There was a roaring in her ears. Her throat constricted. She found difficulty in drawing air into her lungs. She wanted to scream but no sound came.

The ring. It belonged to Hugo's mother. She'd given it to Marina when they became engaged.

*

Hugo! It's Hugo! thudded through her mind. Annalise and Hugo.

The man she'd loved. Still loved.

He was Annalise's fiancé.

*

Throughout the day, tortured thoughts flew through Marina's mind. All this time she knew and she never told me. All the things I told her about our marriage. She listened and never said anything.

Does he know that she knows me? Does he know that the woman whose scarf he chose in Paris as a gift for Annalise's so-called friend was for me?

What would Hugo think if he knew that Annalise was sleeping with Mark? Would he still want her?

Would she care?

What kind of a person is she? Does she have a conscience?

I don't think she has.

I don't think she gives a damn about anyone. Just doesn't care.

My God! What a bitch she is. A real bitch.

*

What about Mark?

Mark was a man Marina liked. Perhaps could even learn to love. But Mark was sleeping with Annalise.

*

That afternoon, he came to her door with a small carved box.

'This is for you,' he said. 'To thank you for last night. I enjoyed the evening.'

She took the gift. Her fingers moved over its geometric patterns.

'Are you okay?' he asked, watching her pale face, her vacant expression.

She did not answer. Instead, 'Do you love her?' her voice wooden, her eyes lustreless,

She knows, he thought. Answered gently, 'Yes. I suppose I do.'

He paused and looked into the distant mountains. 'As much as I'm capable of loving anyone.'

*

Both men were with that hateful woman. Both of them in love with her.

*

Hugo had sat unmoving in his car, his head reeling. Annalise. His fiancée. With another man. The woman he loved. The woman he desired more than any other woman he had known. The woman who'd assured him of her devotion to him. Who held his hand. Who wound her arm through his arm. Who walked in step with him, smiling up at him, her eyes gazing into his, filled with wonder. Who sat close to him. Who held him when they slept, her soft pliant body becoming one with his.

Annalise who whispered to him over the phone and sent kisses, telling him how much she missed him. How she longed for him.

Their trip to Paris. The city of lovers. The city for lovers. Where they declared their love for each other. Where they swore they would be together forever.

Was this the woman with dishevelled blonde curls who'd ardently kissed a tall dark man at her gate? Was that Annalise?

He asked himself how much he know of her. She who came and went. The luscious woman with the blonde curls and glowing eyes and red lips that spoke many loving words?

What game was she playing? Why was she with him? What did she want of him?

He drove carelessly, recklessly, back to the city, these thoughts whirling in his mind. He did not hear the loud hoots of cars, the curses and rude finger signs of truck drivers. He sped, tearing at his steering wheel, his tyres squealing, without thought for himself or anyone else.

He pulled into his garage.

Sat quite still, his face stony, his eyes staring.

*

He remembered the sapphire ring. His mother's ring.

Marina had cherished it. She'd looked wonderingly into its perfect chiselled blue brilliance and said it was the most beautiful thing she'd ever owned.

She cried when she gave it back to him.

'You can keep it,' he'd told her.

But she did not want it. The ring was a symbol of him. Of all that he'd meant to her. If he was not going to be in her life, she did not want the ring.

Now Annalise wore it. His mother's ring that had symbolised love and devotion. Loyalty and honesty. Trust. Above all, complete trust.

It was in a white rage that Hugo reversed the car out of his garage. He was going back.

He would see that woman. Tell her it was over.

Take back the ring.

*

He accused her.

She said he was mistaken. He was a friend. Just a friend.

He said, 'What do you take me for!'

She said that she loved him. Only him. That she would never be unfaithful to him. That she would never have slept with that man! He was just a friend. A mad man who lived on the mountain.

On top of it, he was a Jew! Did he think she would sleep with a Jew? she demanded. 'A dirty Jew.' That's all he was. A mad Jew who lived on the mountain…

If Hugo wanted it, she would never see him again. Not even speak to him…that filthy dirty Jew.

He did not answer her.

'Hugo,' she cried. 'Hugo! Listen to me. Please.'

He demanded the ring.

She held onto it.

'Give it to me,' he shouted.

With tears in her eyes, she took the ring from her finger, looked longingly at it, and unwillingly placed it in the palm of his hand.

*

Hugo sat silently in his car in the parking lot beside the shop.

He took the ring from his pocket and looked at it. Yes. He had it back.

But retrieving it did nothing to diminish the white-hot waves of anger and hatred he felt for the woman he thought he loved. The woman he had so desired, had given up his marriage to be with.

*

Mark stood at the dim entrance of the shop. He saw them, the man leaning menacingly towards the woman.

He heard their loud argument. Listened to her words.

115

Heard how she'd referred to him, the woman that he thought he loved. Mad man from the mountain. Filthy dirty Jew.

*

He whirled around and stormed into the dusk. Mad man. Dirty Jew.

Anger built in him. This was the woman whose bed he'd shared the night before. Who held him and comforted him in his dark times. Whose body excited and warmed him. The woman who made him feel human, connected to the world. The woman who would save him from himself.

Mad man. That's what she'd called him. Filthy dirty Jew.

Those who looked out of their windows would have seen him reeling up the street, his hands pushing through his hair, mumbling incoherently, his dog slinking behind him, ears flattened, tail down.

Alabaster sensed the madness. Was alert and afraid.

Those who watched him drew curtains and locked doors.

They'd heard about Mark. They knew of his madness.

They shrunk into themselves and waited warily in silence.

Her breath reeked of liquor. She stumbled against the counter in her high-heeled shoes as she shouted instructions down the long gloomy interior of the shop. 'Dora,' she yelled, her blonde hair awry.

She'd been drunk before. Had surreptitiously swallowed mouthfuls of liquor throughout the day. Her eyes had become glazed, but never before had she been out of control.

Yesterday was the drunkest Dora had seen her. The black woman had spent the day unpacking goods, cleaning the counters, wiping down the insides of the refrigerators, packing orders, and carrying groceries in boxes on her head in the sweltering streets, dogs growling at the scent of her black body.

She'd returned to the bleary-eyed woman slumped in a chair, her brother confronting her.

She'd heard Frederick say, '*Godse Hemel!* Annalise! You're dead drunk!'

'So what,' was her response. 'So I'm drunk.'

And then, turning to Dora, she'd shouted, 'Where the hell have you been! I've been calling you all afternoon. Calling and calling. You were nowhere to be found. I pay you good money to be here. In the shop. Not fucking in some shack with your boyfriend.'

'*Haai!* Madam!' Dora's hands flew to her face. Her eyes widened in disbelief. 'I was taking the orders to the houses. Same like I do every day.'

'Same like you do every day,' Annalise responded with disdain. 'That's what you say. Same like you do every day. *Ghott!* What an excuse. You people are all the same. We give you jobs and you play with our kindness. You make fun of our generosity. You take advantage at every opportunity.'

'No, ma'am. I didn' take 'vantage. I been working. Taking the orders to the people. Madam can ask them. I make six orders. Take them to the houses.'

*

Annalise staggered to her feet and moved menacingly towards the black woman. 'Don't argue with me,' she yelled. 'I know you people. You're all the same. You pretend to work. And you steal! You're all thieves. You steal all the time. You steal the minute my back's turned. I'm sure you've stolen from the till. Wait until I count the takings today. There'll be money missing. I'll call the police, Dora,' she threatened. 'You'll go to jail.' Spit collected at the corners of her smudged red mouth.

'No, ma'am.' The black woman shrank back in terror. Jail! She'd never been to jail. She'd never done anything that warranted calling the police. 'No, ma'am,' she wailed. 'I nevah took money from the till. I nevah evah done that.'

Her face crumpled. She wrung her hands and in desperation turned with pleading eyes to Frederick. Uncharacteristically, he felt a wave of pity for the figure of the broken woman who stood before him.

'Annalise.' His voice was firm. 'What are you saying? Dora's never stolen from you. You know that. She's worked here for years. You've left her in charge when you were away. She's never taken anything from the shop. In all the years. You know that. What on earth are you saying?'

'I know what I'm saying.' Annaliese stumbled as she stepped away from Dora. 'She's a thief. They're all thieves. These *bladdy kaffirs*. The scourge of the earth.'

Frederick turned to Dora. 'Go, Dora. Go home. Madam isn't feeling well. She'll be better tomorrow.' He called to her receding back, 'Take a package of sausages for your supper.'

And then, thinking that the woman was out of hearing range, he turned to his sister and exclaimed angrily, 'Poor woman. You spoke to her like she was a dog.'

Dora heard him.

She heard Annalise say, 'Well, she is a bit of a dog. Don't you think?'

*

She'd heard all this before. Many times. But she needed the job. She needed the money. She needed the tumble-down shack that she called home. The place she decorated with pictures torn from magazines. She'd swallowed these insults directed at her and her children and her people because she believed that she had no choice.

But 'dog'. That was too bad. Nevah can she be call a dog. NO. Not DOG. She's a person. A human. With same blood in her veins as white people. She can think. She can talk. She is not an animal. She is not a dog.

Veins swelled in her temples. Her head felt as though it would burst. Her body shook uncontrollably. Her hands trembled.

She could not think. She could not feel. She could not speak. She could not hear.

She thought that she would die from the red-hot anger that welled uncontrollably within her.

*

In the cold night air, in the glare of a huge moon, Dora sat outside her shack, enveloped in a blanket that she had weaved in Marina's class.

She was also enveloped with hatred penetrating her soul, penetrating her being. Intense, overwhelming, consuming, hatred.

*

She would never work in the shop again.

She would no longer go to the classes for weaving and knitting. She would not go to the farm house.

She was finished with the white people.

A dog…

She wasn't a dog. She was a person.

They were the dogs.

The dusk did little to alleviate the gloom of the long shop with its one dull globe that glowed weakly, reflecting a small circle of light on the ceiling, but doing nothing for the grey shadows below.

Annalise sat, her high-heeled shoes cast off, her legs spreadeagled, her head hanging forward, chin in hand. Her blonde glossy curls were messed, her eyes dull, her lipstick smudged. There was a hopeless slump in her shoulders, a sagging of her full breasts.

She'd drunk half of the bottle of brandy. The liquor usually worked, dimming the grim shadows that lurked ominously in the distant corners of her mind.

But now those images kept coming. A blue-eyed child with a mop of sunny curls, hopping, jumping, laughing as she was thrown into the air and caught against her father's broad chest. Snuggling with glee into his neck.

'NO!' screamed inside her. 'DON'T!'

Splashing. Soap bubbles, blowing soap bubbles in the bath. Daddy wash me. I wash Daddy.

Daddy hold me in front of him on the horse.

Daddy hold me in front of him in front of the steering wheel.

NO! DON'T!

Daddy teaching me to dance.

Ma watching us, disapproving, smoking a cigarette, saying nothing. Ma was scared of him.

They all were.

Except me. I was never scared of him. I never had to be scared. He loved me. Looked after me. Held me close. My daddy. He loved me.

I was his favourite. That's what he said. I could do whatever I wanted. I could have whatever I wanted. Just stamp my lttle foot and he would smile and throw me in the air. What does my little girl want, he laughed, tickling me.

NO DADDY DON'T!

It's not right, they said. The way he carries on with Annalise.

*

I don't care. I don't care what they think. I will take what I want when I want it. That's how I was brought up.

I don't care who gets trampled on in the process because that's how I am. Annalise. Beautiful Annalise.

Heartless?

Maybe.

But I don't care.

*

Who cared about me?

Who really cared about that small child with the blue eyes and the tumble of sunny curls? Who said NO! ENOUGH! She's just a child. You can't do that to her!

NO ONE!

No one cared. Not my mother, not my big brother Frederick. No one cared.

So why should I care about other people?

Why should I care about the men who claim to love me! They only want from me what my father wanted.

I don't understand what they mean… Love me…

What is love?

What does love mean?

And the women! Did my mother protect me? NO!

Women deserve to be hurt by me. They deserve my spite! They deserve to be damaged as I was damaged.

They represent my mother.

My mother who did nothing to save her little girl.

Let them all suffer.

*

She took another swig from the bottle, coughed and swallowed.

*

There's something wrong with me, she told herself.

I'm ill.

My body feels swollen. My mind is jumbled. Perhaps I'm dying? Is that bad?

Perhaps I'll find peace in death? I haven't found it in living.

*

Perhaps I'm asking for death from all the people I've hurt. Perhaps that is why I hurt them.

So that they will hunt me down and kill me.

*

Her head fell forward.

She vomited over her scarf and down her skirt and onto the floor. Brown vomit formed a stinking mess around her feet.

Unsteady, groping for something to hold onto, she pulled herself up and lurched barefoot down the dark narrow length of the grim shop.

To where the sacks of potatoes lay, and the giant pumpkins.

There, among the dusty sacks, she knelt on her hands and knees, then fell face forward and slept with the smells of onion skins and dried garlic, in the acrid damp of brown vomit.

It was an unseasonable time for a gathering of clouds. Over the ranges, the fog surged, obliterating sculptured rock and pine thickets in impenetrable grey mist.

The eagle perched on its rock with folded wings. The yellow eyes of owls were shuttered. Larks were silent. Snakes coiled. Meerkats huddled. Tortoises pulled in their heads. The quills of porcupines lay flat. *Grysbok* became statues.

The sky heaved. In the distance, an ominous rumble of thunder. Leaves danced dervishly in restless funnels of air.

A dog whined.

Cats crouched, their eyes staring.

Something unusual was happening in their world of blank bland days when the predictable sun moved across the skies, stirring life in them with the warmth of its rays.

Something strange…

*

Frederick instructed the men to bring in the cows, the sheep and the horses.

Women took washing off the lines, latched garden gates and drew curtains against blinding shafts of lightning.

*

Storms were also broiling in the hearts and minds of Lettie, Marina, Dora, Mark, Hugo.

They had been provoked.

Violent and uncontrollable eruptions were surging within them.

*

The clouds were dense and black.

Lightning flashed like flint rapiers. Terrifying thunder followed. Then the rain.

Fierce and powerful.

Impenetrable walls of water bending all to their will.

*

But despite its ferocity, there were those who defied it.

Shadowy figures found their way and were each on their own alone with Annalise.

No one knew who had tightened the scarf around the drunk woman's throat. It could have been any of them.

*

Now she lay, face down, at the back of her long dim shop among the giant pumpkins and sacks of potatoes.

A French scarf in an artwork of colours suffocatingly wound around her full white throat.

Marina crouched on the floor before the dead fire, the only light a glow from the tip of her cigarette. She drew on it frantically, coughed and exhaled, feeling in her pocket for the packet she'd grabbed from the shelf as she ran from the shop, then falling, bruising her hands and knees, then onward over broken ground until she reached her door and stumbled into the dark room, collapsing into the horror of that dark night.

The long dim passageway, the smell of spices and kerosene, the shelves she'd brushed past that seemed to want to take hold of her, the frantic thudding of her heart.

The woman who lay shapeless among the sacks of potatoes, her scarf painted into that lifeless space.

The scarf from Paris.

She lit another cigarette from the stub of the previous one. A wave of nausea came from the pit of her stomach.

But despite her shock and her shaking body, Marina felt vindicated.

Annalise deserved to die. She needed to die.

Whatever the consequences, Annalise had to die.

*

In the house next door, the fire crackled and flickered, casting ugly shadows on the walls.

Like the waiting pile of logs, Lettie waited, heavy legs firmly planted, folded arms branched from her solid shoulders. Her eyes were lifeless coals, her face stone.

In her lap, her large square hands clutched, big fingers intertwined. Strong capable hands.

Hands capable of…

She'd not stumbled when she left the shop. Her large feet stepped surely on the rutted pavements, her stocky body was steady, her mind cold and clear.

That woman who'd threatened to expose their daughter, deny her a chance of White education, would never threaten her again.

Annalise – the woman she detested – needed to die.

*

In the black night, a tall figure strode across the veld. The dog, Alabaster, filled with foreboding, brushed against its master, wanting reassurance.

The man was unaware of the dog.

He moved automatically, unaware of the black skies – an ominous canopy that stretched to the mountains.

Words drummed in his head.

Mad Jew. Ugly Jew. Dirty Jew.

Those words from the woman he'd thought he could love.

She'd betrayed him, the woman he thought would bring him back to life.

Golden Annalise of the riding bracelets and glittering diamonds, her crimson fingernails moving suggestively over his body.

Annalise, with her soft yielding body and whispering words, who'd found a chink in his impregnability…

Needed to die.

The dog whimpered, then howled, as it loped along, desperately trying to brush life back into its departing master.

*

Dora sat on a stool outside her hut, her blanket huddled around her shoulders.

There was no light from her brazier, no moon or stars. In the far distance, the mournful howl of a fox.

Or was it a dog?

Dora had been called a dog.

Cold seeped from the ground into her feet and up her legs. Her face was cold. She tightened the blanket around her. Her arms encircled her thin body. Her hands clutched at her ribs.

She sat in the black night, waiting to understand. Lwazi, fingering the scar that ran down the side of his face, knew about the white madam. He'd told her what needed to be done. He'd threatened to do it for her.

She'd told him, no, she did not want that. Her son was in enough trouble. She told him to leave. 'Now!' she'd screamed at him. 'Go now!'

In the black night, she heard his words. They echoed in her head. It was as though he was sitting next to her.

Now she understood.

Impatiently, she shook the blanket from her shoulders. Her mind was focused. Surges of energy pumped through her body.

Yes. The white woman must pay for calling her a dog.

She must pay.

She must die.

*

Hugo drove back to the city along the long lonely road. His hands held the wheel lightly, his head was light and clear.

Annalise needed to die.

The woman he loved. The woman who'd betrayed him, who'd deceived him with her wiles and her lies and her creamy beauty and her soft kisses and the fire that burned within her, who'd given light and warmth to his life – had needed to die.

He felt in his pocket. The sapphire ring was there.

He drove along the dark roads untroubled by black fields and the outlines of black mountains against a black sky.

No moon. No stars.

The world was a black veil.

As he neared the city, the first grey of a gloomy dawn lined the horizon.

There was the sound of sirens. A police van and two police cars zoomed past him.

They were going in the direction of the woman who lay lifeless among the sacks of potatoes.

Marina had thought to go back to the city. She'd sit on her stoep with her coffee and cigarettes staring at the veld, at the distant mountains, thinking that she should pack her belongings, contact her brother, and drive away from the potholes without looking back.

Days became weeks. Then months. All the while, she sipped coffee and blew smoke.

On a cold winter's morning, she tied her hair back and went to her workbench. Feverishly she worked through the long dry days and endless nights, moving from room to room in the house in Bluegum Street, surrounded by a disorderly mass of materials and piles of unfinished work, stubbing butts into overflowing ashtrays and leaving a trail of stained and unwashed mugs.

They came to her exhibition. 'Not the same,' they complained. 'Uninspiring. Dull. No vision.' She overheard their words. 'She used to be so creative. She's lost it.'

She forgot to eat. Her wrist bones protruded and her shoulder blades jutted under her sweaters. A hoarse and persistent cough never left her.

'You'll get a cancer from those cigarettes,' Lettie said.

She did not tell Lettie she was coughing blood.

*

Lettie and Gert had no reason to leave.

Their daughter who Lettie had forbidden to attend an Afrikaans school had avidly learned the language from her grandmother. She'd also learned to love the elderly woman who bought her clothes and pretty pieces of jewellery, gave her an Afrikaans Bible and took her to the Suid Afrikane Gereformede Kerk on Sunday mornings. On Sunday afternoons, she sat at her grandmother's table with gracious Afrikaans ladies whom she called Tannie, drinking tea from bone china cups and eating cake with dainty silver forks.

When the time came, it was no surprise that she chose to go to an Afrikaans university. It was also no surprise that the pretty accomplished girl would marry well, to a successful barrister from a prominent Afrikaans family.

Their circle of friends conceded that although it was obvious she had a 'touch of the tar', she was refined and elegant, well educated and, most importantly, had made an excellent match.

The daughter was fulfilled but she was also painfully aware of her Coloured background and would do everything to obliterate that terrible shame from her past.

She rejected her mother. Wanted nothing to do with her.

She would have nothing to do with any person from her mother's family.

Gert and Lettie remained in their house in Bluegum Street. There was no reason for them to leave.

*

During the night of Annalise's murder, Mark disappeared into the mountain. For a while, Alabaster tried to keep up with him. But there were sheer cliffs to climb, and the dog kept falling back, until, disillusioned, with head down and tail between legs, it gazed in the direction of its departed master, then sadly moved away.

Alabaster moped for many days. Wandered around the cathedral of trees, ears pricked for any sound that could be Mark, any scent of him. Became skin and bone. But eventually the dog began to thaw. Caught a wild rabbit and tore at it with sharp teeth. Drank copiously from the clear clean stream. Wandered over the mountains.

One day, a farm worker claimed to have seen Alabaster loping through the veld. He told them he called out. The dog had stopped and turned to face him. The worker said that Alabaster had growled threateningly and bared its teeth.

The worker ran away. He was afraid. He said that the dog had turned into a wolf.

*

There was no sign of Mark.

No one ever knew what happened to the man on the mountain.

Whether he was alive or dead.

No one bothered to find out.

*

Dora remained in her hut.

Frederick was told that she'd lost her mind.

She seemed possessed. Mumbled to herself. Threatened anyone who came near her. Ate from the bins.

Was dirty and ragged except for one item of clothing – a silk scarf that was tightly bound around her head. A scarf she's found in Marina's bin, flowing colours bold and true.

On a freezing winter's day, Dora took to a bedraggled corner of her hut, her ravaged body tightly wrapped in a blanket.

She remained there. Not stirring.

Until the blanket became a shroud.

*

The first thing that Hugo did was to sell the sapphire ring. He felt relieved to be rid of it.

He tried to resume his practice, but was unable to concentrate. Allowed deadlines to pass. Missed appointments. He did not care.

He bought a one-way ticket to France and searched until he found a place for himself – a small villa in a mountain village.

He made a living supervising repairs for crumbling farmhouses bought by Englishmen and Americans who wanted to experience life with the locals in the vineyards, surrounded by olive trees.

*

The police had come.

They'd searched for clues. Taken fingerprints. Taken photographs.

They tried for many months to find the person who'd perpetrated the crime.

*

To this day, the murder of Annalise van Rooyen remains unsolved.

www.ingramcontent.com/pod-product-compliance
Lightning Source LLC
Chambersburg PA
CBHW021203110726
47900CB00002B/706